T0161341

The Amorous Intrigues and Adventures of Aaron Burr

The Amorous Intrigues and Adventures of Aaron Burr

Anonymous

MINT EDITIONS

The Amorous Intrigues and Adventures of Aaron Burr was first published in 1861.

This edition published by Mint Editions 2021.

ISBN 9781513132686

Published by Mint Editions®

 **MINT
EDITIONS**

minteditionbooks.com

Publishing Director: Jennifer Newens
Design & Production: Rachel Lopez Metzger
Project Manager: Micaela Clark
Typesetting: Westchester Publishing Services

Contents

I

The renowned Aaron Burr was a standing argument against the old saying, that "none but fools fall in love with women." This talented, heroic, and energetic man was an adorer of the fair sex. From the age of puberty to the day of his death (which occurred in his eightieth year), Aaron Burr was keenly alive to the fascinations of the fairer portion of creation, and esteemed their smiles as sunny rays darted from heaven.

It is reported of him, that he had "a flattering tongue," but that is probably a vulgar prejudice. Let others try the flattering system, and they may find that, in a majority of cases, they will only be laughed at for their pains.

It is more probable that Burr felt all he said—that he praised women because he adored them, and they knew he was in earnest. It is well enough for men who are feebly endowed, and whose love for women is at best lukewarm, to attribute to heartless flattery the success which they have vainly sought to obtain, and which is readily due to a genuine love for the charms of woman.

We are not, however, apologizing for the faults of Aaron Burr; we shall only aim to give him his due; and we shall also do justice to the charms of woman, when we remember that Burr was neither a fool nor a poet.

He was no dreamer, who invested the fair sex with the bright creations of a vivid fancy, but a man of sound, cool, and accurate judgment, keen discrimination, and one who possessed great knowledge of human nature. As a lawyer he was pre-eminent, and as a statesman he had no superior. He was a man of great benevolence, and impoverished himself by his liberality to those who stood in need of pecuniary aid; but among the women, it must be confessed, that he was often led away by the warmth of his temperament.

The infancy and boyhood of Aaron Burr passed under the most favorable circumstances. They were such as to give him an exalted opinion of that sex which is so capable of imparting to us the keenest enjoyments, both of a physical and moral nature. He associated with none but respectable young ladies of family and of education.

The grandfather of Burr was a German of noble lineage, and his father, the Rev. Aaron Burr, was educated at Yale College, and was subsequently appointed the President of the New Jersey College, known afterwards as Nassau Hall.

President Burr, father of our hero, was married, in his 38th year, to the daughter of Jonathan Edwards, the celebrated metaphysician and divine. President Burr was celebrated for his eloquence and his piety, and was also noted for his eccentricity.

The mother of our hero, Esther Burr, thus speaks of him in a letter to her father, President Edwards:

> "My little son (then twenty months old) has been sick with
> the slow fever since my brother left us, and has been brought
> to the brink of the grave. But I hope, in mercy, God is
> bringing him up again."

Aaron not only recovered, but possessed a good constitution, great muscular power, and an independent, self-relying mind. This he evinced by running away from his preceptor, when only four years of age.

Aaron Burr was born on the 6th of February, 1756, in Newark, State of New Jersey. His father died in August, 1757, and his mother during the following year, leaving two children, Aaron and his sister Sarah. Sarah married Judge Tappan Reeve. Colonel Burr inherited a handsome estate on the death of his father.

Although deprived of his pious and highly respectable parents, Burr fell into good hands.

Aaron and his sister were transferred to the family of Timothy Edwards, their mother's eldest brother, who lived in Stockbridge, Massachusetts.

In 1762 Mr. Edwards removed to Elizabethtown, New Jersey. A private tutor was engaged for Aaron and his sister, Judge Reeve occupying that station for a considerable time.

When ten years old, Aaron ran away from his guardian, and went to New York for the purpose of going a sea voyage. He engaged himself on board a vessel as cabin-boy. He was pursued by Mr. Edwards, who found him on board; but the young hero was determined not to be taken until he had made terms of peace with his guardian, and ran up the rigging to the top-gallant-mast head, where he remained till he had received a promise that he should not be molested, if he returned home.

In the year 1769, Burr entered Princetown College, where he soon distanced all competitors, and gave ample proofs of an o'ermastering intellect. He was sixteen years of age when he graduated, and received the highest academic honors that the faculty could bestow.

No doubt the pure life led by Burr, under the tutelage of the good and virtuous, contributed much to preserve his intellectual faculties in all their force, and as he was never led into any improper habits, he retained his vigor till he was old enough to go into society, and form attachments for such of the fair sex as pleased his taste.

From the best authority to which we have recourse, we believe that Burr never gratified the sexual passion till he was seventeen years of age.

There was, in the neighborhood of Bethlehem, Connecticut, a girl of eighteen years, named Adelaide King.

Burr, who appears to have had some concern to the subject of religion about the time he left college, and some months afterwards, called upon Rev. Dr. Bellamy, who lived at Bethlehem. This was in the autumn of 1773, and there he first saw Adelaide King.

Adelaide had not had the advantage of a strict or a genteel education. Her father was a man of taste, but he paid little attention to his family, and the mother and child may be said to have run wild, and to have paid little attention to appearances. Perhaps it was for that very reason that Adelaide drew the attention of Aaron Burr. Her total want of affection, united to extreme beauty, both of form and feature, and the most soft and feminine manners, combined with the brusque style of the "Nose" school, interested him exceedingly.

There was something so original in a beautiful, tender-hearted girl, expressing brilliant sentiments in the unadorned and unaffected manner of the lower orders, with the occasional use of a slang phrase in musical tones, and coming from the sweetest lips that were ever formed, that Burr listened to the conversation as if it had been the tone of an angel's lyre.

Careless of her dress, she was yet cleanly, and appeared to Burr more engaging in her village bonnet and checked apron, tripping on the green, than the ladies of refinement whom he had known, attired in "silks and satins new."

With a small waist, Adelaide had rounded, voluptuous hips, full calves, and a small foot. Her limbs were, indeed, models for the statuary. Her eyes were blue, and peculiarly expressive. A kind and gentle heart manifested itself in all that she said and did; though there was no mawkish sensibility, no pretension to feeling, nor, indeed, pretension of any kind.

While with one ear Burr listened to the ghostly teachings of his reverend friend, the other was open to the harmonious tones of the entrancing Adelaide. It would appear that the latter carried the day. The priestly divine was no match for the divine Adelaide, who so fired the imagination of young Burr, that he could think of little else during the latter part of his sojourn in Bethlehem.

Burr had become acquainted with Adelaide King, at the parties of the young, which were then held with little regard to precedence. Nearly all classes mingled in the dance, the ring-play, and the corn-husking. It is true that Burr was not expected to form acquaintance among the common people; but having seen Adelaide at church, he made the necessary inquires, and found that she might be met with once or twice a week at the parties.

It does not appear that Adelaide observed the young student till he met her at the house of a Mrs. Lewis, who had several daughters of her own. Though she must have met him sometimes in the road, he did not particularly attract her attention. Perhaps this may be accounted for by the fact that Burr's appearance was that of one of the members of the upper class, and Adelaide was not troubled with worldly ambition. She seemed satisfied in her humble sphere. Besides this, Burr was small in stature and in frame, and women generally notice men of larger growth.

No sooner, however, had Burr addressed her at the house of Mrs. Lewis, and shown by word and looks that he admired her, than Adelaide became fully sensible of the honor done her.

The Misses Lewis had given a party, and as young men dropped in on such occasions, without waiting for "an invite," Burr made his appearance among the rest.

The girls, generally, knew Burr by sight, as young man of wealth and talent cannot make his debut in a country village without occasioning a flutter among the gentle sex.

When Burr entered the room, every eye was turned upon him. The plays partially ceased, and there were earnest whisperings among the pretty girls for some minutes.

Finally, however, the ring-play went forward again with spirit. A ring is formed by the company, who pass around two or three lads or lasses in the centre, singing some popular song. At the conclusion of the singing, those in the centre choose partners from the ring, when they kiss, and the latter then take their places in the centre, and choose in turn.

They began to circle around him, singing:

> *"Come, Philanders, lets be a marching,*
> *Every one speaks from his heart-string,*
> *Choose your true-love, now or never,*
> *And see that you do not choose any other!"*

The eyes of the girls glistened as they were turned towards young Burr, each one hoping to be selected by the "gentleman," but they were not left long in suspense.

Reaching forth his hand, Burr seized that of Adelaide King, and drawing the beautiful girl to him, he pressed her plump bosom forcibly to his own, and inflicted a dozen kisses on her dainty red lips.

As soon as Burr left her to take his place in the ring, Adelaide blushed deeply, cast down her eyes, and sighed. It was evident that the honor of being chosen by Burr was wholly unexpected by the young beauty, while the ardor with which he embraced her, testified to the peculiar admiration with which she had inspired him.

This choice was unexpected by Adelaide, because she did not know how beautiful she was, and because there were other girls present, whose fathers owned large farms, and who felt themselves above her. She had supposed that young Burr would, at least prefer the wealthiest people in the village, where all were below him in social position. But the fact was, that Burr could perceive little difference between villagers, save in beauty and intelligence. Those who possessed the largest farms, were sometimes the most deficient in those qualifications.

The plays continued till three o'clock in the morning, and often did Burr lead Adelaide into the centre of the ring, and inhale the sweetness of her virgin charms, though he sometimes choose others for the sake of appearances.

Between the plays, Aaron continued to place himself by the side of Adelaide, and found a singular charm in her conversation, and the untaught grace of her manners.

"How exceedingly white and pretty your hands are!" said he. "Can it be possible that you do any kind of work?"

"I spin, sir, and I card wool," returned she, looking down at the hand which he had extolled, and turning them over for examination, as if she had never before observed any thing peculiar about them; "and I wash, and husk corn, and do many other kinds of work, sir. But," added she, smiling, and exhibiting as she did so the loveliest pearls, "some say that women's work isn't nothing; but it's so constant!"

"Constant! Yes, that's natural," returned he, "for constancy is a great virtue in a woman."

"Oh, yes, constancy is very good, but that is very different from constant work."

"But constancy leads to constant work, sometimes, I should think," said Burr, laughing.

"Yes, sir, when they get married. Though we all work in the country."

"Who do you think is the prettiest girl in the room?" said Burr.

"Penelope Shattuch has that name—the girl in the pink frock yonder, talking to the tall young gentleman."

"What, she! Why, her form is not much."

"I don't know. Here they say that beauty consists in black eyes, red cheeks, and a slim figure."

Burr burst forth into shouts of laughter, which quite astonished Adelaide.

"My own sweet seraph!" cried he, "there's not a girl in the room who can compare with yourself, and you have neither black eyes, red cheeks, nor a slim—Ah! yes, you have a small waist undoubtedly, but otherwise you are full; with the most enchanting bust that nature ever fashioned."

"You think so, sir? I don't think that I am handsome."

"Then you pronounce me no judge of beauty! I hope that you err on that head, at least."

"Oh, no, I wouldn't be willing to tell any gentleman that he is no judge of beauty—"

"Ay, ay, I understand. You only think that I am fond of deceiving and flattering the ladies—of speaking what I do not think."

"Oh, no, by no means. Not that, but—"

"But what? Why do you pause?"

Well, I don't know—only, I never was called handsome."

"Then it is high time that you were. Many homely girls have been told that they were handsome, and it is a hard case if one so beautiful as you must never hear the truth."

By this kind of conversation with Adelaide, Burr made more progress than he was aware of, for Adelaide was not one of those girls who are easily led to express their feelings; nor was she ready to believe that Burr was in love with her.

It was enough that she soon knew she was in love with him, whether he was sincere in his profession of admiration for her or not.

This, then, was the first love adventure in which Aaron Burr was engaged. He was seventeen years old at the time.

Long years have passed since then, and long years had passed at the time of Burr's death on Staten Island, since Adelaide King had been consigned to the old grave-yard of Bethlehem. Yet Burr never could hear the mention of her name without emotion. There was something so real, so devoted in the love of Adelaide for Burr, that he never could think of her without a pang, even after so many others had been added to the list of his conquests.

It was down in a green lane, some half a mile from the village church of Bethlehem, in a valley of palms and daisies, that Adelaide King yielded up her virgin purity to the importunities of her lover. The very spot has been pointed out to us more than once.

There, with the beautiful and tender Adelaide in his arms, Burr quaffed the sweetest joys ever vouchsafed to man, while the glorious form of Adelaide was thrilled with raptures that she had never before imagined.

Again and again did they rush into each other's arms, till nature was exhausted, when they parted with one long-continued kiss.

"Dear Adelaide, for ever dear, we shall meet again."

"Yes, Aaron, beloved of my soul, we shall yet be happy. You will return soon?"

Thus did the lovers separate, she to return to the roof of her parents, and he to repair to New Jersey, where he took up his residence with his brother-in-law, Tappan Reeve.

There was evidently a correspondence kept up, for a short time, between Aaron Burr and Adelaide King, after the return of the former to New Jersey.

It gradually languished on the part of Burr, and Adelaide, doubtless warned by the tenor to his letters, soon gave up all hopes of seeing him again. The following appears to be her last letter:

DEAR AARON

You say truly that the opinion of the world must be consulted in many of our most important actions. Had

I consulted that, instead of my devotion to you, I should not now be in a way to become a mother, but not a wife. Should the poor little creature live, who is now bounding in my bosom, as if it knew I was writing to its father, may Heaven shield it from the disgrace which will be heaped upon its mother as soon as it is born. But you love me no more, and I need not write again. Farewell, Aaron! I shall trouble nobody long.

A.K.

Her words were prophetic. The child was born, and Adelaide was turned out of the house by her parents. She did not let Burr know this fact, but took refuge with her child in the alms-house among the "town poor." There she was kindly treated by Mrs. Armstrong, who had charge of the poor at that time, but grief and anxiety for the fate of her child brought on a fever, which carried her off in a few days. Her child survived her only a week.

Burr knew nothing of these things, but was waiting to hear from Adelaide, that he might send her money. At the same time, he had never dreamed that her parents would turn her away from her home. The parents knew not who was the father of the child, as Adelaide had never mentioned the name of Burr.

When, at length, Burr learned the fate of Adelaide King, he was thunderstruck. Though he kept his own secret, except that he imparted it to his friend Ogden, and one or two other intimates, yet there was observed in him a change about the time of this tragedy. His ardor in the pursuit of the fair sex did not at all diminish: his happy experience with Adelaide, led him to desire the society of the opposite sex, though he had never thought of returning to the gentle maid of Bethlehem, because he was in no haste to marry. Still she dwelt in his thoughts, and he could never think of her without a sigh of regret; and when he heard of her death, it affected him deeply, and wove into all his after life a dark thread, which gave a sombre tint to the whole tissue.

This was, however, a great secret hidden from his wife; and when, long afterwards, Burr had become a noted warrior and politician, on the isle of la Belle Riviere, where Mrs. Blennerhassett surprised him in a deep reverie, and asked him what sad memories engaged his attention, he immediately replied:

"The Babe of Bethlehem!"

To this the lady replied that she was glad to find his mind so devoutly employed.

He smiled mysteriously, and said, with a deep sigh:

"But it is I who suffer the crucifixion."

Mrs. Blennerhassett often related this anecdote as an evidence that Burr was capable of religious impressions. Alas! had she seen the following scrap, found in an old volume of Plutarch's Lives, she would never have given currency to so great an improbability:

> *There came in the twilight gloaming,*
> *A mournful cadence o'er the lea:*
> *"Poor branded Cain, where art thou roaming?"*
> *A plaintiff voice saith unto me.*
> *"Is it thy voice comes through the glade,*
> *And is't thy voice so softly sighing,*
> *The mournful tones of Adelaide,*
> *And her poor, houseless infant dying?*
> *"Those distant recollections fade,*
> *And can I still be aught to them?*
> *The young and beautiful betrayed,*
> *And her poor babe of Bethlehem!*
> *"Oh! wander on, thou lonely man,*
> *Through the thickets—*

Here the manuscript broke suddenly off, and the paper was also blotted, as if the writer had relinquished the idea of finishing the piece, and thrown it aside. It suffers, however, to explain the meaning of Burr's reply to Mrs. Blennerhassett.

It was not Bethlehem of Judea, but Bethlehem of Connecticut, the residence of Rev. Dr. Bellamy, to which Col. Burr alluded.

We write thus to show that Burr, though a reckless seducer of female virtue, was deeply sensible of the worth and devotion of Adelaide King, the beautiful maid of Bethlehem.

II

DESCRIPTION OF BURR.—A BEAUTIFUL GIRL.—LOVE AT FIRST
SIGHT.—UNTIMELY VISITOR.—REV. DR. BELLAMY IN NEW JERSEY

After his return to New Jersey, Burr at once became famous as a
gallant. His height was just five feet six inches; of a handsome
though slender figure, and possessed of a great muscular power. He
could also endure great hardships and fatigue. His carriage was very
erect and dignified; his forehead was broad and high, and his hair dark,
and worn behind in a queue. His nose was nearly Grecian, and his
mouth had an expression of voluptuousness, deceit, and cunning. His
chin was broad and well-moulded; and his eyes were large, black and
penetrating—once seen, never to be forgotten. This magnetic power
was great, as many of the gentle sex knew to their sorrow.

His daring, independent spirit recommended him to the ladies, who
admired courage and independence, very generally, and it was not long
after his return, that he had a convincing proof of this, which gratified
his vanity exceedingly.

Aaron was one day walking in an unfrequented spot (for there were
many wild and solitary places in those days), when he saw approaching
him a lady on horseback.

Without appearing impertinent, he took measures to ascertain
whether it was a young or elderly rider. His stealthy glances soon
convinced him that she was both young and lovely. She was not above
the middle size, and of feminine proportions and features, yet there was
a certain *hauteur* in her bearing which only rendered her more interesting.

As the rider drew near, Burr perceived that she was dressed in rich
and fanciful style. She wore a riding-habit of blue cashmere, with
yellow buttons, and the cuffs and collar were composed of red velvet.
Her scarlet velvet cap was trimmed with fur, and sat very gracefully
and rather jauntily on her head, while from under it fell a profusion
of jet-black curls, which Solomon would have compared to clusters
of ripe grapes. Her stately neck was of the purest alabaster, and her
lips, like threads of scarlet, only opened to disclose pearls of surpassing
whiteness.

Her bosom was plump, and of a good size; the shoulders faultless.
The taper waist was admirably contrasted with well-rounded hips, and

her manner was graceful—nay, fairly bewitching. She carried her head with an air of pride and gentleness combined, which stamped her a member of the upper classes of society.

Our hero looked more than once at this charming rider, but when she drew very near, he was about to pass with a simple bow, when her lips parted, and in musical accents, she inquired:

"Pray, sir, do I not address Mr. Aaron Burr?"

Burr started with surprise, but soon recovered his self-possession, and replied:

"My name is Aaron Burr, Miss. Can I serve you in any way?"

"I beg your pardon sir," she said checking her horse, and blushing deeply; "but you have forgotten me doubtless?"

"I must have seen you before," said Burr, "though your name has slipped my recollection; nor is it strange, for my memory is very defective in the matter of names and dates."

"Angelina Dudley," said she with a sweet smile.

"Ten thousand pardons, Miss Dudley!" cried he, with animation. "I recollect you perfectly well. It was at the house of—," he paused, for he had, in truth, no recollection of ever seeing the young lady before, and her name was entirely new to him. But the young lady helped him out; for perceiving that he hesitated, she cried:

"At the house of Lord Stirling."

"Oh! forgetful dolt that I am!" resumed Burr. "I remember it was there—I—I—I—danced with you—"

"No, sir!" interrupted Angelina, laughing merrily; "we did not dance on that occasion, and as I said little, you may have but a very indistinct recollection of me; but, sir, I observed *you*, and was much pleased with your remarks on the subject of the aggressions of the King and Parliament."

"I am glad to hear—"

"Oh! sir, your patriotic sentiments found an echo in my heart!"

"You do me great honor, Miss, and this certainly the happiest moment of my life."

"I am glad that you are happy," said she, in a mournful tone.

"May I not hope that Miss Dudley is also happy? Ah, were she, indeed, as happy as she is beautiful—"

"Oh, sir!"

"Nay, I do not flatter. You know that I speak the truth. I do not believe that a lady is to blame when she is beautiful for being conscious of the fact."

The emotions now betrayed by this fair interlocutor, let Burr into her secret. She was silent several moments, evidently endeavoring to commanding her feelings.

"Will not Miss Dudley descend and let her horse crop the beautiful grass and clover? It will be to her an agreeable change to walk a little."

"Thank you, sir," said Angelina, as Burr assisted her to alight, and took charge of the horse. He took the bit from the mouth of the animal, who was soon engaged in devouring the daisies and butter-cups, while Burr took the hand of Miss Dudley, and kissing it, said:

"To form an acquaintance with Miss Dudley, would be the most fortunate circumstance that has yet brightened my existence."

"To try to dissemble any longer, would be sheer folly," cried Angelina. "You see the state of my heart; but pardon—Oh! pardon the unwomanly step which I have taken, and despise me not; but ever since I met you at the house of Lord Stirling; I have been most unhappy."

"And yet you have taken the trouble to see me again! If seeing me once made you unhappy—"

Angelina laughed through her tears at this sally, and then placing her hand in that of Burr's, rested her cheek upon his shoulder, and giving vent to her long-suspended feelings, sobbed aloud.

This was an interesting situation for a young man like Aaron Burr to be placed in. It was very much as if a young sheep had reclined upon the bosom of a lion, to enjoy the tender sympathy of the king of the forest.

Burr put his arm around the waist of Angelina, and pressing her to his throbbing heart, applied his lips to those ivory globes which rounded up over her dress, almost to the nipples.

The effect of this was instantly apparent. The warm-hearted girl sighed heavily, there was a choking sensation in her throat, and her large dark eyes were rolled up in her head with such a softness in their expression, that Burr must have been more or less than man, not to have desired a more intimate acquaintance with her.

"My dear love!" cried he, kissing her furiously, and throwing her back upon the grass, "you are as lovely as a seraph!"

He threw up her clothes, and revealed such charms as seldom have been exposed to the light of the sun. The smooth, round belly, the voluminous yet compact thighs, the robust calf, and small foot and ankle, the satin smoothness of the skin, and other graces not to be mentioned, but whose pouting and moist freshness betokened a guarded virginity, which, however, longed for the pressure of manhood, all these so fired him with passion, that he had scarcely the necessary patience to prepare himself for the amorous encounter.

Just as he was about entering the gate of Paradise, the snorting of a steed was heard. Both of them started. Burr looked towards Angelina's horse, and saw that he was silently feeding by the way-side. He could not have made the noise. Burr sprang to his feet, and looking beyond a projection of the road, beheld his worthy friend, the Rev. Dr. Bellamy, riding towards the spot, with saddle-bags, umbrella, and the other accoutrements for a journey.

The reverend gentleman was close upon the enamored pair, and there was not a moment to lose; Burr raised the young lady to her feet, smoothed down her dress, and taking a book from his pocket, began walking along by the side of the girl, as if discanting upon the contents of the volume, in conjunction with the beauties of nature.

Angelina understood this manœuvre, and acted her part as well as she could, but her countenance was very pale when Dr. Bellamy came up. The latter recognized the youth immediately, and reined in his steed.

"You here, doctor!" exclaimed Burr. "I am right glad to see you!"

He then seized the doctor's extended hand, and pressed it cordially. The doctor expressed himself highly pleased at the encounter.

"All in good time," said he. "I was on my way to the house of your uncle, my friend Edwards, and you can point me out the exact spot, for I must confess that this region is entirely new to me."

At the same time, the reverend doctor glanced at Angelina, who had sunk down upon a rock, and at her horse, who was enjoying the largest liberty among the long grass and wild flowers.

"This is Miss Brown," said Burr, quickly; "she has experienced a fright: her horse ran away with her—"

"Indeed!" cried the doctor, innocently. "He seems quiet enough now. Are you not afraid to trust him alone?"

"Oh, no sir, he sometimes gets frightened, and runs, after which he is quite docile. I fear that the effects of Miss Brown's alarm will be serious; if you will permit me to get some water—"

The doctor eyed the young man closely.

"You were reading a volume to her—"

"Oh, yes, sir!" cried Burr, who perceived that he was caught. "I was telling her to be composed, and read something to her which was calculated to confirm her trust in the protecting care of Divine Providence."

"I am glad to find that the hours you spent in my library have not been without their good fruits," said Bellamy. "You have then become a sincere believer, at least, in an over-ruling Providence?"

"I think it good policy to refer those to the 'good book,' who have been educated in its precepts, like Miss Brown," said Burr, "as I would refer a Mahometan to the Koran—"

"But, pray, get the water you spoke of for the young lady, who may be suffering while we discuss theological questions," said the doctor.

"The devil! What sent the old curse here just at the critical moment?" said Burr to himself, as he led Angelina to a neighboring brook, and dashed the pure water over her temples.

Burr took this opportunity to whisper to Angelina that he would get clear of "the old hunks" as soon as possible; but she was too much agitated to make any reply, except by deep and frequent blushes.

The disappointment had evidently been quite as severe to Angelina as to Aaron, perhaps even more overwhelming, and she continued faint and haggard.

As Dr. Bellamy now rode up to the spot where the lovers stood, Burr began to describe to him the house of Mr. Timothy Edwards, and the roads which he must pursue; but it was not easy to make the reverend gentleman comprehend the way, and he found that he could not get clear of acting as a guide to the worthy clergyman, without an open show of disrespect, and in those days, a regular minister of the gospel was "some pumpkins."

Burr, therefore, asked Angelina if she felt able to ride.

"By no means," cried the doctor. "The young lady must not be trusted on the horse again. We will accompany her home first. After that, you can go with me. How far does Mr. Brown live from here?"

This was putting a new face upon the matter. Angelina had no desire to be seen by her family in company with Burr, and the story of a frightened horse would sound very strangely in the ears of her father, who knew that Angelina was a fearless rider, and that the pony was gentleness itself.

"There is no necessity," said the disappointed girl, quickly; "if Mr. Burr will have the goodness to assist me in remounting the horse, I will manage to get home myself."

Burr sighed, but he saw no other way. He did as requested, and Angelina set out on a slow trot for her father's house. Burr then obtained a horse in the neighborhood, and guided the Doctor to the mansion of his worthy relative.

III

NIGHT WALKING.—A ROUGH ENCOUNTER.—A YOUNG LADY
FROM NEW YORK.—A MAD BULL IN CHURCH

On the way to his uncle's house, Burr conversed with Dr. Bellamy about the troubles, that were then becoming serious, between Old England and the Colonies: but the doctor was evidently disposed to turn the subject upon youthful follies and indiscretions, and he glanced so often at such matters, that Burr entertained little doubt that his course with Angelina was suspected by the old gentleman.

Under the circumstances, the interview between Burr and the doctor was far from agreeable to the former, who left his old friend as soon as decency permitted, and rode back to the spot where he had assisted Angelina to mount her horse, being impressed with a vague hope that she had lingered about the spot, or had returned to it, with the hope of meeting him again.

Burr was doomed to be again disappointed; for the beautiful dell, in which he had encountered the lovely girl, was deserted by all but the birds, which sang their roundelay, as if endeavoring to cheer the unhappy youth; but their music failed of any such effect.

He remained on the spot till long after night-fall, and then, as some alleviation to his anguish, he determined to walk across the plains, to the house of Mr. Dudley—a distance of five miles—and endeavor to catch a glimpse of the beautiful girl through the window, or even obtain an interview with her, if the thing were possible.

"That she loves me is certain," said he, as he walked briskly forward, "and if she has not returned hither, it is because she is afraid of behaving to bold, especially as I have tried to go to extremes with her. If she returned, she thinks it would appear as if she had come back for the express purpose of throwing away her maiden-head. Therefore I must make all advances in future. As for old Dr. Bellamy, I shall hereafter regard him as one of those stumbling-blocks, who will neither enter heaven themselves, nor suffer others to go in when they have an opportunity to do so."

When Burr reached the grounds of Mr. Dudley, he met with a reception that was far from flattering. While crossing a meadow that lay between him and the mansion he heard hasty steps thundering behind him, and on turning his head, he saw through the darkness, the form of a large white horses approaching. The animal came on as if enraged at the young man's intrusion upon his premises, and with the evident intention of trampling him under his feet.

Burr rushed towards the infuriated steed with uplifted hands, and words of stern command; but the animal was not to be frightened by such opposition. He showed his naked jaws, and thrust out his head to bite, while, at the same time, he struck with his fore feet.

If our hero had not darted behind a tree, he would have been roughly handled. The beast persisted in following him up, and Burr caught up a large stone, but unwilling to injure the animal, he did not immediately throw it. He looked about him for a fence, over which he could escape, and at that moment, the horse caught the collar of the youth between his teeth, and tore it from the body of the coat. Then the exasperated lover struck at the animal with the stone. The horse reared, and made a plunge at him,and when inevitable destruction seemed to threaten the young man, the wayward beast wheeled, and ran off at full speed to the other end of the lot.

"A narrow escape!" said Burr, aloud, and he walked forward till he came to a stone wall, which he clambered over only to find himself in the close vicinity of a large dog. The animal made a rush at him, yelling hideously, but he was fortunately chained, and could not quite reach the spot where Burr stood.

The noise made by the dog quickly alarmed the inmates of the Dudley mansion, and Burr heard the doors open, and a cry of "thieves! thieves!" from some half a dozen voices.

Burr dodged back over the stone wall, while footsteps of his human pursuers sounded nearer and nearer. He had got about half way over the meadow, when the thundering hoofs of the white horse were again heard in his rear. Horse and men, the latter with loud shouts and imprecations, followed fast after the youth. He saw no other way but to trust to his good legs, and he thought only of flight. He exerted himself to the utmost, and at length gained the fence. He bounded over the rails, and the horse came no farther; but the men kept up the chase. A thick, black-looking grove lay on one side of the flying youth, and towards this he now directed his steps. He was soon among the under-wood, and pricked himself severely with briars. At the next moment, he slumped up to the middle in a quagmire. He thought himself a captive, but the darkness favored him, and though one of the pursuers passed very near, and probably saw him, yet he might easily have been mistaken for the stump of a tree, as not more than three feet of his person was standing out of the mud.

Be that as it may, all the men rushed by, with threatening cries and ferocious yells; and Burr, by clinging to the branch of a staunted hemlock, which extended over his head, succeeded in regaining solid ground.

He then ventured to walk forward over the fields, but narrowly escaped falling into the hands of his pursuers on their return. By throwing himself flat on the ground, amid a forest of whortleberries, he eluded their observation.

Though he had undergone some peril and no little fatigue, we are sorry to say that Burr went to bed, that night, neither "a sadder" nor "a wiser man." He resolved to make an attempt to see Angelina on the next night, by approaching the mansion in front.

Burning with impatience, Burr thought the sun marched in the wrong direction, and would never reach his western goal. But evening at length came on, "and twilight gray had in her sober livery all things clad."

Our hero secured a sharp dagger about his person, and with a stout staff in his hand, set out on foot for the mansion of the Dudleys. When he reached the white pailings which enclosed the front door-yard, Burr found that the lower rooms were well lighted, and the sound of merriment within announced that there were visitors in the house.

Our hero waited a long time without catching a glance of her whom he sought through the lighted windows, though he saw the dark forms of men occasionally, as they passed by the casements.

At length, the company began to retire, and Burr hid himself till the sound of their rolling wheels could be no longer heard.

He then came forth, and saw a light passing through towards the upper part of the mansion. Then he beheld the form of Angelina at the window. The night was hot, and the sash was raised.

Burr whistled to attract her attention, but Angelina did not seem to hear the signal. He whistled again, and she leaned out the window, looking anxiously towards the spot where Burr stood. He was then determined to pronounce her name; but the word died away upon his lips, as he saw the front door open, and a gentleman appeared with a lighted segar in his mouth. The gentleman remained in the porch, smoking, some minutes, and Angelina, in the meantime, extinguished her light.

"She has gone to bed," said Burr to himself. "How vexatious!"

At that moment, a bright idea flashed through the brain of the young adventurer.

"I will write to her," said he. "I will conjure her in the most solemn manner to meet me in the same spot where we encountered each other before. I will promise to be most prudent, and will profess the most devoted love—that will do. At least her answer will show me what she intends to do."

Burr went home, sad and disconsolate. He had never felt more miserable, and he declared to himself that life was nothing but a hell upon earth.

The next morning, Aaron went down stairs with a heavy heart, but he very unexpectedly encountered, at the breakfast-table, a beautiful blonde, a Miss Edwards, from New York, a distant relative, who had formed an acquaintance with his sister in the metropolis, and who had now called to make a visit of several days.

Burr's head was so full of Angelina Dudley, that he saluted the young lady from New York with formal politeness. He listened to her conversation during breakfast, however, and found her lively and intelligent. Withal, the glances she now and then cast at Aaron, were well calculated to satisfy his vanity, of which he had no small share, when women were concerned.

He then regarded Miss Edwards more attentively. He saw that her locks were flaxen and very abundant; her complexion was pure; and bust good, and her form very voluptuous and elegantly turned. Her hands and feet were small.

By degrees his imagination became fired, and before night, he said many soft things to the white-bosomed maid of Gotham.

Alas! the letter to Angelina Dudley was not written that day; he would do it early tomorrow morning.

The morning came, and Aaron was in a hurry to join Miss Edwards; he would write to Angelina in the evening. By the time evening arrived, the letter was forgotten entirely: he had kissed the lips of the handsome blonde, and found them sweeter than the honey of Hybla.

Mrs. Reeve was not altogether ignorant of the roguish propensities of her promising brother, and evidently watched the growing intimacy of Aaron and her lively visitor with some suspicion. She was determined that Miss Edwards should not suffer an irreparable injury to her house, and frequently broke in upon the tete-a-tetes of the young couple, with visible manifestations of uneasiness.

Aaron saw that he must set his wits at work, and one Sunday, when the trio set out together to church—Mr. Reeve being from home—the former feigned a sudden faintness, and the good sister went back for her salts, leaving Aaron and Miss Edwards in the centre of a piece of woods. Aaron lost not a moment, but commenced the violent protestation of undying love.

Miss Edwards and Miss Dudley were two very different women, and the former had not, like Angelina, made the first advances. She received kindly the declarations of Burr, and evidently regarded him in the light of an honorable suitor, which she inwardly thought he was. When, therefore, he hugged and kissed her, she only sighed and gently disengaged herself from his grasp; but when he proceeded to assail her bosom, she struggled hard to get away, and told him to wait until he could honorably claim what he now seemed disposed to wrest by force. So long did the young lady resist her enterprising lover, that Mrs. Reeve returned with the smelling-bottle, before he had made much progress in his lawless attempt.

Mrs. Reeve discovered nothing peculiar in the appearance of the youthful pair. She supposed, by her visitor's blushes, that Aaron had snatched a kiss during her absence, but nothing more.

At church, Burr was surprised to see Angelina Dudley. She was not accustomed to attend that house of worship, but had come, on the present occasion, to hear a new preacher, who had exchanged pulpits with the clergyman who usually officiated there. She sat in the pew adjoining the Reeve's family.

As the eyes of Angelina and Aaron met, a deep blush suffused the countenance of the enamored girl.

Aaron exchanged several glances with Angelina during service, and read in her countenance something which he did not quite understand. She was very attentive to the words of the speaker.

Just as the service was concluded, a loud noise of men and boys was heard in the vicinity of the church.

All listened, and the service was suspended a few moments, when a mad bull rushed furiously in at the open door, and passed down the aisle of the church. Many rushed from the building, and among them Mrs. Reeve.

Great was the confusion. The bull bellowed and tossed his horns; some ran up the pulpit stairs, and others fled to the doors and windows.

In the melee, Aaron Burr found himself standing near an open window, between Angelina and Miss Edwards. Both of these young ladies looked to him for protection, with fear and anxiety vividly depicted on their countenances.

The bull was plunging directly towards them. There was time to seize one of the young ladies, lift her up, and thrust her through the window. Burr must instantly decide which of them to save.

In this dilemma, our hero perceived that his chances with Miss Edwards was sacrificed for ever, if he gave Angelina Dudley the preference.

Accordingly, he caught the former in his arms, and put her out the window, where hands were ready to receive her half-fainting form. Angelina, giving her supposed lover a look of astonishment, sprang over the railing of the altar, and just escaped the horns of the enraged animal. Burr himself was knocked down and slightly bruised, but sustained no other injury.

Perceiving that Angelina was safe, Burr turned towards the bull, but the discharge of a couple of muskets, in the hands of men from the outside, settled the whole affair by giving the cause of all this trouble his quietus. It appeared that no body had been hurt by the bull, though clothes had been torn in clambering out of his way, and several ladies had been seriously injured by fright.

IV

The Letter to Angelina.—The Sick Neighbor.—
Pursuit of Pleasure Under Difficulties.—Burr's Ready
Wit and Powers of Invention

When Burr retire to his chamber on that Sunday night, he could not help reflecting on the events of the day, and particularly upon his conduct towards Angelina. What must she think of his neglect to save her from imminent danger, from his desire to protect another? Had he not shown her plainly that he had forgotten her, and, worst of all, would she not suppose that he despised her for the bold step that she had taken, in conferring her partiality for a young man, which she felt before he had spoken to her.

"She shall not think that at any rate," said Burr, and before retiring to bed, he sat down, and wrote her a long letter.

He protested that, in the hurry and confusion of the moment, he had mistaken the young lady whom he had saved for Angelina, and that the former was an individual towards whom he was entirely indifferent, while for Angelina herself, he entertained the most fervent love, the most entire devotion.

"Without you," he added, "I shall be entirely miserable; without you, most beautiful of women, I live in a barren desert, joyless and desolate. Meet me, if you care for my happiness, for my life itself, on the very spot where I first encountered you. I promise to be prudent. Only let me hear again from your divine lips that I am not an object of indifference to you. I need not name the day, for I shall be there every day after three o'clock till you come."

Burr put this letter in the post-office, and waited four days for an answer, visiting the place of assignation every afternoon.

No answer came, and he waited in vain in the pleasant dell where they first met. In the mean time, his attempts on Miss Edwards were continued. She was deeply grateful for his noble conduct at the church, and called him the preserver of her life; but they were closely watched by Mrs. Reeve, and the time drew near when the fair visitor must return to New York.

Having been so cruelly baffled in the affair of Angelina, Burr felt that he must expedite matters with Miss Edwards. It was too much to be disappointed in both instances.

Fortune enabled him to procure a private interview when he least expected it. A neighbor was taken suddenly ill, and sent for Mrs. Reeve. That lady lost no time in answering the call, but the neighbor lived three miles off, and she should be absent two days.

Miss Edwards must not be left alone with Aaron at all that time. She, therefore, engaged the young lady to follow as soon as the chase could be got ready, and to spend the time with herself at the house of the sick neighbor. As for Mrs. Reeve, she accompanied the messenger in a vehicle that would only hold but two persons.

Aaron overheard this arrangement, though he was supposed to be out of the house. As soon as his sister was gone, he presented himself before Miss Edwards, and said:

"That old chase! What! ride in that broken-backed concern when the walking is so beautiful! I know that Miss Edwards is incapable of such folly. Come, get your hat and shawl; I will go with you. We will have a splendid walk."

"Agreed!" cried the gay girl, running for her "things," and putting them on.

They were soon on their way to the house of the sick lady.

"Yes, dearest Adele," cried Burr, as soon as they were clear of the house, "my feelings towards you have undergone no change. The more I feel your sweet presence, the more I am penetrated with your beauty and amiable, lovely nature."

"Oh, Mr. Burr! you have brought me out here to talk love—I know you have. Now, suppose that I should refuse to budge, till you promise to—to—be reasonable."

"Now, Adele, can you pronounce it irrational to love, and to love such a one as yourself? Oh! then I am indeed mad—stark, staring mad—for never was I so overwhelmed, so touched to the very centre of the heart, by feminine excellence and beauty."

This conversation was continued till they reached the spot where Burr encountered Angelina Dudley, and by that time, the fair listener had became deeply affected by the protestations of the man who had saved her life, and who she had, indeed, learned to admire. As yet however, Burr had suffered her to suppose that marriage was his only object: when they reached the "valley of love," as Burr called it, the latter paused, and while Miss Edwards leaned heavily on his arm, he pressed her to his heart, and kissed her lips. She did not resist, until he attempted a second embrace. She then said:

"There, Aaron, that will do for the present. We are alone, remember."

"Would that we could always be alone," cried he, passionately; "that we had a solitary island, where no human foot-step but our own could intrude; that I could see thee, only thee, light of my soul! most glorious, beautiful, and gentle one!"

In pronouncing these flattering words, Burr gradually pressed her closer and closer to him, and as she drunk in the welcome words, her resistance became feebler and feebler, till she became powerless, and dropped in his arms.

He laid her on the grass, and she sighed heavily. He hastened to tear open her bosom, and apply his lips to those ivory globes, whose fragrance fairly maddened him. He threw up her dress, and then she became suddenly aroused, as if a serpent stung her, and would have cast him off; but he was the stronger of the two. She tried to scream, but the sound died away in heavy sighs and choking sobs.

She smarted a moment, and gave a low shriek, but soon the most thrilling raptures entranced her.

She forgot all prudence, all shame, and only knew that she was wrapped in elysium, dissolving in a sweet flame of transport. She threw her plump limbs over him, strained him to her bosom, and both were alike eager in tasting all the bliss they could seize.

Just then a gentle step on the green sward might have been heard, had the lovers been less intent upon devouring each other with kisses and amorous struggles. A beautiful maid was on the spot; she heard sighs and tender words rapturously expressed. She came around the corner of a high bush, and beheld a scene that transfixed her to the spot. Burr turned his head, and Angelina Dudley stood before him!

She, poor girl, had but just received the letter written by Burr, and had hurried to the appointed place, only to find her "devoted lover" administering comfort and consolation to a rival beauty, with all the zeal and vigor of which he was capable.

Finding himself fairly detected, and that his duplicity must become manifest to both of the young ladies, Burr finished his business, and, starting up, said to Angelina:

"Come, my dear, now it's your turn! Lie right down!"

Angelina stood gazing at Burr and his companion, the latter being at last sensible of the presence of a third person.

Adele hastily adjusted her clothing, and regained her feet, but feeling that her reputation was compromised, she sank back upon the earth in a swoon.

"Was it for this that you sent for me?" said Angelina to Burr. "Oh! is it thus that you mock my too, too constant love?"

She covered her face with her hands, and wept.

"I mocked you not," said Burr; "but so long a time had elapsed since my letter was sent, that I despaired of hearing of you again. I supposed myself deserted for some happier man, and though I loved not this lady who lies before us on the ground, yet my thwarted love drove me mad, and as my pent up passions must have vent, I merely used this girl, as one would use a common stroller, to cool my blood. Having utterly despaired of hearing again from you, what better could I do?"

Miss Dudley listened, and was glad to believe that Burr spoke the truth. She permitted him to toy with her bosom, until, overpowered by her feelings, she sank lifeless in his arms. In another moment she lay upon the ground, and he had forced the gate of love. He had driven away all impediments, and Angelina, in her turn, experienced those first raptures which so overcome the virgin heart of woman.

Burr found Miss Dudley far more warm and animated than Miss Edwards. He tasted the sweetest draught that he had ever known, while she swooned away with the agonies of untold bliss.

Just as this passionate couple reached the climax of enjoyment, and while they breathed fast and loud, Adele recovered from her swoon, and raising her head, saw Angelina struggling with bliss in the arms of Burr, until she fainted with the excess of pleasure.

Miss Edwards bounded to her feet, and as Burr regained his, she confronted him with staring eyes and pallid lips:

"How—how is this? What girl is that? Is it thus you prove your devotion—your constancy—"

"Hush, my dear!" cried Burr. "You now perceive that your reputation is safe. Yon fainting girl, who discovered us by sheer accident, would have made the whole country wring with the news, if I had not stopped her mouth by stooping her—other end. Now, you perceive that you have her reputation in your power, and you both stand on equal ground. She cannot tell of you, nor can you tell of her. I saw that there was no other way to insure secrecy, and, therefore, I had recourse to this method, though I can assure you that I have done it wholly on your account. I have thus saved your good name."

It is said that "there is no evil without its good"; and Miss Edwards felt that if her lover had been inconstant, he had certainly saved her good name. The awful fear of exposure which had caused her to faint was removed, and a dreadful weight was removed from her mind.

Angelina soon recovered her recollection, and Burr then whispered to her that he was obliged to accompany the other young lady to her place of abode, but begged her to call upon him on the next day, at the same place, when he would explain everything.

Angelina sighed and retired behind the bushes to conceal her blushes, while Burr and Miss Edwards walked slowly forward. They had one mile farther to walk, through some fields and swampy places where there was much underwood.

Having made sure that Angelina had not followed them, Burr again pressed the bosom of Adele, and she soon yielded to his blandishments. He laid her upon a grassy hillock, and again unveiled her alabaster beauties. This time she made little resistance, even to the last act of love. She had tasted sweets that were too alluring to be rejected when offered to her, and now she quaffed the cup of bliss with a readiness and an earnestness of manner which bespoke both a warm and a vigorous constitution.

They then arranged their dress and hair, and pursued their walk till they reached the house of the sick lady, where they found Mrs. Reeve. That lady regarded them both with a scrutinizing glance, and although she made no remark, she had her private thoughts.

V

Meeting of Angelina and Her Lover.—Stirring Scenes.—Honorable Sentiments of Burr.—Lovely Character of Angelina

Having deposited Miss Edwards at the house of the sick neighbor, Burr bade her farewell, and saw her alone for the purpose, in the porch, Mrs. Reeve being at the time in the sick chamber.

The enamored girl, who had been initiated into those sexual joys which so enthrall the heart of a young, buxom woman, threw her arms around our hero, and kissed him vehemently. She called him by every endearing name, told him that he had caused her the highest gratification, and that she should worship his very name to the last day of her existence. Such were her feelings then.

Again and again she made him return, after he had addressed himself to his journey, that she might kiss his mouth, neck, and cheeks, and press him to her swelling heart.

Finally the adored youth tore himself away, and went home.

On his way to his sister's house, Burr reflected upon what had passed. While he acknowledged that Adele Edwards had uncommon claims to admiration, and that her form was cast in the finest mould, he could but feel that Angelina Dudley was more exquisitely beautiful then her rival, and that she was capable of imparting more pleasure to the man of the heart than the other could do.

Angelina was evidently of a warmer temperament. In the intercourse which our hero had enjoyed with her, she had thrown her whole soul into the act: she had been too much entranced to think of any thing else but her lover, and the means of increasing the pleasure by the action that nature dictates in such cases. She was desperately amorous, and Burr compared her to a live coal of fire. He panted, therefore, for a second interview with her, when they could meet free from those embarrassing circumstances which had interfered with their raptures on the previous occasion.

Unfortunately for Burr, it rained hard the next day, and he knew that it was of no use to go to the trysting-place in such weather. His impatience and chagrin were such that every hour seemed an age. He watched the clouds to see if he could not discover an appearance of breaking away, but the sullen heavens continued black and lowering, and the rain was falling fast, when at eleven o'clock he retired to bed.

Burr slept soundly, however, and when he opened his eyes at a somewhat late hour, he beheld the bright sun shining in at the casement. He now feared that Angelina would not come—that some untoward accident would prevent her from making her appearance.

But he knew not the nature of Miss Dudley. Having once tasted those pleasures which had overwhelmed her soul, and maddened her with the most flaming passion for the beloved author of her joys, nothing but death could have prevented her from repairing to the happy dale, so sacred to the memory of unexpected bliss.

Although Burr went early, he found Angelina waiting for him. She had seen his approach at a distance, and had hidden behind a tree.

Burr reached the spot, burning with impatience. Casting his eyes around him, and not doubting that he was entirely alone, he mused aloud, while Angelina, within five or six feet of the spot where he stood, could distinctly hear every word that he uttered.

"Heaven and hell!" cried he; "she is not here. But it is early; I could not hope that a lady would precede me. But if she does come, won't I give her a specimen of what a man can do! Won't I make her sweet body writhe like a skinned eel! I will again see her beautiful eyes grow soft and fill with transport—with tenderness! They again will roll in her head with delight; her beautiful mouth ajar—her sweet breath—her heaving bosom—and such a bosom! How lovely she is! Oh! what a woman! How well formed for loving! Her limbs too! Those legs, those thighs, that smooth belly, and that heavenly spot, with the glossy threads—I'll devour her alive! But oh, my God! suppose that she will not come—"

"But she will come!" exclaimed a musical voice, and Angelina darted out from behind the tree, where she had been hidden, and flew into the arms of her lover.

"Ten thousand—thousand thanks! sweet man!" exclaimed she, "for the proof of your love. I have now heard you praise me when you thought you were alone, and could have no motive for practicing deception! Oh! my adored Aaron, I am yours, yours for ever, and I will love you—I will adore you, sweet, dear, dear blessed angel that you are, to the latest day of my existence."

Then she fell to kissing him, as if she was determined to devour him alive.

"I have been so impatient for this moment!" said Burr.

"Not more impatient that I have been," said she, throwing her arms around his neck again. "When I woke up yesterday, and saw that it rained, I felt as if my heart would break. All day I was miserable but this morning—ah! that atoned for all. I thought—I—I—thought—ah! ah! ah!"

The break in Angelina's last sentence was caused by the fact that her lover was applying his lips to her plump and fragrant breasts. This caused her such tender throes of pleasure that her utterance failed her and she could only breath soft and musical sighs—her balmy breath perfuming the very air around them. Determined not to be interrupted this time, Burr took her sweet body up in his arms, and conveyed her to a secret recess in the center of the bushes and underwood. Here they could not be seen by any chance passenger.

Natural modesty caused Angelina a little resistance, when Burr threw up her dress so far as to completely expose her most secret charms. He then caught one hasty kiss of the plump and silky "mons veneris," and plunged between her smooth and ample thighs, like a fiery warhorse rushing into the battle. For a moment modesty prevented Angelina from exhibiting the pleasure which she felt; but it was too sweet—the gushings of rapturous joy immediately became too intense to permit her to remain passive.

Then, with eager warmth, she threw arms and legs over her lover, and entwined him in a most fervid embrace answering to his motions with equally lively ones of her own. She sighed—she writhed—she cried out with transport—she fastened her mouth to his—she murmured and exclaimed:

"Dear, dear Aaron! My life! My sweet! My heaven! Adored one! Worshiped angel! Oh! heaven! Oh! transport! Oh! I shall faint! I shall die! I am on fire! I can't bear any more!"

Then, when the climax arrived, she gave a shriek, a deep, long sigh, and became entirely lifeless in the arms of her ardent lover.

As this sweet embodiment of heavenly beauty lay panting on the green sward, Burr threw himself on her bosom, kissed her lips with furious passion—kissed her beautiful lips, her bosom, and every glowing charm that she possessed. Oh! it was a banquet fit for the gods!

Burr declared that, until then, he had formed no idea how exceedingly lovely a woman could be—that his passion seemed to increase, even by indulgence.

"And this specimen of God's choicest workmanship loves me," said Burr to himself. "I never knew happiness till this moment."

Burr dashed some water in the face of the prostrate angel, and she opened her sweet, dark eyes.

"Oh!" said she, in a murmuring tone, "I am in Paradise! Kiss me, love. Press your lips to mine, and let me die in your blessed arms. You have made me so happy! Good heavens! what a sweet thing a man is! You have overwhelmed my soul with sweet, heavenly fires. Oh! that you would press me and love me to death. I want to perish amid the rapturous flames that you kindle in my glowing body. Inexpressible joy!" cried Angelina, pressing his head against her naked bosom.

Then Burr, in his turn, broke out into vehement professions of everlasting regard—extolling her charms, and dwelt upon their peculiar attractions—kissed her bosom—her neck—her swelling hips, her belly, her thighs, and with maddened eagerness, tasted the fragrance of all her voluptuous beauties.

Passion swelled high in their young veins, and again the burning lover forced his way into the gate of Paradise.

They cling to each other, they sigh, they devour each other as the fiery rapture increases, and with the climax, lie lifeless in each other's arms!

That was a day of joy and transport to the two lovers, and when, at length, they bade each other adieu, and separated to return to their respective homes, their parting was sincerely tender on both sides. Burr perceived that he had found a congenial being in Angelina, whose lively nature and ardent temperament agreed well with his own, and rendered her peculiarly pleasing to him. He determined to treat her with respect, and to study her happiness.

"Though I may never marry," said he, "yet Angelina Dudley shall never have cause to repent her acquaintance with me. I will be her friend, as well as lover. May God in heaven bless the dear angel!"

VI

THE YOUNG WIDOW OF FIRST STREET.—THE HYPOCRISY
OF BURR.—TEMPTATION, FALL, AND SUBSEQUENT DISTRESS

As Aaron Burr had some business to attend to in an adjoining colony, which could not be neglected, he had told Angelina Dudley that they should not be able to meet again under a week. He promised, however, that he would write to her.

He then set out for New York. His business detained him longer than he had expected, and he had been some ten days in the Empire City, when one of the most remarkable events of his life occurred. As this affair is connected with the history of his intrigues, we will endeavor to recount the whole story as it happened.

On a Sunday evening, Burr was sauntering about the streets, and ogling the ladies, when he chanced to hear the singing of a church congregation in his vicinity. He followed the sound till he came to a substantial Methodist meeting house, and having nothing else to do, he dropped in, and took a seat with the rest.

A remarkably eloquent preacher was, at that time, holding forth, having just commenced his sermon. Burr listened attentively, and the stirring discourse of the reverend gentleman appears to have made some impression upon his feelings. The singing which followed was very animated, and being one of those lively tunes common among the Methodists, was to Burr a rarity.

Among those who sang was a young lady, who sat not far from our hero, and her voice could be distinguished from those of the other singers, being peculiarly pure, rich and melodious. Her hair was black as the raven's wing, while her blue eyes were large, and fringed with long dark lashes. As her lips parted, they disclosed small white teeth, very evenly placed. Her features were not of that precisely regular form which is supposed to constitute a perfect beauty, but the whole expression of her countenance, animated as it was with devotion, pleased Burr exceedingly, and he could not keep his eyes from her countenance.

We may as well say, in this place, that the beautiful devotee was a Mrs. Keating, a young widow, who had lost her husband a year before the time mentioned. Her husband was a young man of education and well bred, but had become reduced by his father's failure in business, and at the time of his death was a thriving cartman, being constantly employed by our wealthiest merchants. Mrs. Keating had no children by him. On his death-bed, young Keating became much concerned about his future welfare, and a very pious and devoted member of the Methodist persuasion held frequent interviews with him. The scenes in the chamber of death made a lively impression upon the sensitive and naturally intelligent mind of his weeping bride, and especially an exhortation which her husband delivered to her just before the closing of his earthly career.

All the warm feelings of her young and enthusiastic heart which had been given to her husband, the young widow now merged in aspirations for celestial purity and those joys which fade not away.

She became a constant attendant upon the services at the Methodist church, and as her religious zeal was tempered with the utmost amiability and gentleness, she drew the attention of the old professors, all of whom held her in high esteem.

Burr regarded her earnestly as she sang, and when the services closed, and she was about to rise, the partial falling off of her shawl revealed to his gaze a bust of the most beautiful proportions.

If he had received any good impressions from the discourse and other services, it is certain that the sight of this engaging woman soon obliterated them from his heart, or left just enough of their gentle and chastening influence to render him more dangerous to such a being as Mrs. Keating than he would have been without it.

Burr kept his eye upon the lady till he had got into the street with the rest of the congregation. He walked along behind her in the throng till she turned into First street (now called Chrystie), and then he fell back a little lest he should be suspected of following the woman.

She pursued her way up First street, which was thinly settled, and the houses very soon became few and far between. He then ranged up alongside of her, and said politely:

"Excuse the freedom of a stranger, madam, but I would say that we listened to a fine discourse this evening, one which will not soon be forgotten."

The lady was a little startled at first, but soon recovered herself, and replied:

"I am glad to hear you say so, sir. You were then at our church this evening?"

"I was madam. I have heretofore been rather remiss in my duties, in that respect, but shall hereafter endeavor to be more regular in my attendance upon religious worship. Not only the sermon, but the singing also is calculated to revive in one's memory the sacred precepts of a dying mother, which are too apt to lie slumbering in one's breast."

"Alas! sir. You have lost your mother! Was she pious?"

"None more so, my dear madam, and," added Burr, speaking in a husky tone, "it was a certain resemblance that I trusted in your voice to hers, while singing, that so powerfully brought back to me the recollection of those days which are passed, and which can never, never return. Some inward monitor seemed to tell me that a few words with you would have a beneficial effect upon my poor tempest-tossed soul, for I have been, first and last, much troubled in my mind on account of religion."

"Thank God for it!" cried she, earnestly; "as it is in that way that God works to bring you to himself. But I fear you have applied to a very weak and unworthy counsellor—"

"Something tells me no. Early deprived of both my parents, I am keenly alive to the blessed influences of the society of virtuous females, especially when they are so beauti—pardon me, madam, I was about to bestow a stupid compliment; but it was out of season, for what is the most angelic beauty when compared with inward graces? And I am confident that even if you were a more ordinary woman in personal appearance, you would be just as happy, so that you could

> 'read your title clear
> To mansions in the skies.'"

The lady appeared to feel that her personal charms had been highly complimented by one who had not intended to say any thing about them, but who had accidentally let out his real opinion of her feminine graces. Therefore, she did not immediately reply; and when she did so, she was careful not to allude to the last words of her companion.

"I hope, sir, the impressions which you have received at church from the discourse of our minister, will not be obliterated. Mr. S. is not only a great speaker, but he is also a very benevolent man—good to the poor and to everybody. He has no pride."

"I should have known that, dear madam, by his looks. Oh! that I were but half as good as he is!"

"That prayer may be more than answered," said the gentle being at his side, in such tones of sympathizing kindness that Burr inwardly cursed himself for a scoundrel; "for we are told that those who hunger and thirst after righteousness shall be filled. But Mr. S. is far from setting himself up as a model for others. He feels that whatsoever he is, it is only by the free grace of our blessed Lord that his feet are preserved from stumbling. We are all impure in the sight of Him at whose feet the brightest angels continually cast their crowns; and as for the poor creature who now addresses you, she is at a stand to decide whether you should come to her or she should go to you for religious instruction. You are certainly a very tender-spirited young man, and show contrition for your neglect of religion heretofore, while I am often hardhearted, and have been sensible that I did not always feel as a christian should towards those who still dwell in the darkness of sin. But here is my home—"

"This then is your house? Ah! madam, after listening to your blessed counsels thus far, can I—must I part so very soon? I fear to go back into the world—my faith is weak, and some few more explanations that I desire—"

"Is it even so, young gentleman? Then, in God's name, walk into my poor tenement, I see that Nancy is still up, and if she were not, God forbid that I should deny any one who comes to me in the name of my Saviour! And may the opportunity be blessed alike to the strengthening of your faith and of mine, for I need it equally with yourself. Walk in."

Burr entered the humble domain of Mrs. Keating, which he found very neat and clean. A large over-grown girl of some eighteen years, was snoring melodiously on a settee, while the candle was flaming in the socket on the mantle-piece.

"Nancy! Nancy?" cried the lady of the house.

No answer. Nancy was in the land of dreams, perhaps toying with her beau, and could not think of leaving such good company to return to the world of cold realities.

"Let her sleep. She is tired no doubt," said the lady, putting a fresh candle in the place of the one that had burned out.

The conversation was renewed. Burr led the way to such topics as were of a melting, soul-subduing character, and ingeniously interwove his religious aspirations with half disguised compliments to the widow herself. Her countenance glowed with feeling, and her lovely bosom rose and fell while Burr talked, and darted into her eyes the tremendous magnetic influence which shot from his own whenever he chose to launch his lightnings at the female heart.

In the midst of their discourse, the sleeping Nancy awoke, sat up on end, glared wildly about her, and perceiving that Mrs. Keating had company, lighted a candle, and staggered off to bed in an upper chamber.

Burr and the lady were now left alone; and by stealthy approaches he had at length succeeded in convincing the lady that he loved her with a pure, exalted passion, at the same time that they were fellow-travelers on the road to Zion.

The young widow possessed warm and tender feelings: her husband had been taken sick before the honey-moon was in its wane, and for a whole year she had not even received a kiss from one of the opposite sex. Her feelings rose higher and higher, till the swelling tide had began to overwhelm her reason. Burr's arm was already around her waist, his lips had touched the sweetest and most beautiful bosom that ever fired the soul of man, when she suddenly became conscious of her awful position!

But Burr had expected this: he was on the watch for it; and he had also read in her gentle heart the fact that she was of a forgiving temper, and that nothing could induce her to peril the welfare of a handsome youth, whose only fault was that he loved her to well—for, alas! she knew not the cold, calculating brain which accompanied that fiery heart.

I say that she suddenly became aware of her danger, and started as if her guardian-angel had cried to her in thunder tones:

"Beware!"

In the very moment that she endeavored, with sudden consciousness, to spring from his embrace, and with a mighty effort had writhed from his grasp, Burr threw himself on her exposed breast, and caught the bright red nipple in his mouth. Here he seemed fastened as if for ever, and devoured the fragrance of that white bosom with as keen a relish as that of the Arabian traveler when he quaffs the waters from a well in the burning desert.

All the feminine fire and tenderness of Mrs. Keating at once returned, and though she still strove to free herself, yet she sighed heavily, and her struggles became weaker and weaker. She sank upon the carpet, and Burr threw aside the envious drapery that concealed charms which might have seduced a man of ice.

The cluster of raven threads which heavily covered the mount of Venus, contrasted beautifully with the white round belly and large alabaster thighs, while the two breasts stood up hard and firm, the lovely neck invited his eager lips, and the blue eyes rolled with wild desire and tender impatience.

We need not mention the sequel. Imagination can hardly paint their mutual bliss, which was intensified by respect and admiration.

No sooner had the first transports subsided—no sooner had they risen from the floor—than the heart of the gentle and loving widow was rent with the keenest remorse. Yet it was not on Burr that she launched her censures.

"It is myself," said she—"my guilty self, who am wholly to blame. I know that men are passionate, and cannot always control themselves. But I, who am older than you—I, who have had experience—Oh, sir, it is a fine monitor, a fine advisor that you have chosen! A fine example I have set a young and hopeful Christian! Now is my ruin sealed, for never more can I lift my guilty eyes to thy throne, oh my God! Let the mountains fall now—"

"Cease! cease! dear madam! Angel! blessed woman!" cried Burr. "Accuse not yourself! we have only been led away by our feelings. You are young and I am young. Is it strange? You lost your husband while you were in the day of life, and nature—yes, nature itself required relief. No one can ever know—"

"There! there!" cried she pointing upward—"there in yon high heaven, is One who knows!"

Burr stopped her mouth with kisses, and forced her to the floor, when the act was repeated, which so completely enkindled the fervent passions of the lovely widow, that she thought no more of any thing but Burr and his embraces.

She hugged him to that angelic bosom, and murmured the sweetest and tenderest words of love, and their blissful dalliance ceased not till the gray dawn gave signal for separation.

Then Burr took his leave, and left the widow, overflowing with tenderness and sweet recollections, to her repose. She sank to sleep, indeed, but fearful was her waking!

No tongue can describe the heart-rending remorse which seized upon that lovely but betrayed being when she woke from her sleep, and remembered the events of the preceeding night.

But we shall speak of her again. We must now follow Aaron Burr to the mansion of Judge Reeve in New Jersey.

VII

ANGELINA AGAIN.—A NEWSPAPER ARTICLE.—AGITATION
OF BURR.—THE WIDOW KEATING

O n the day after the events recorded in the last chapter, Aaron Burr
returned home to the dwelling of his sister, Mrs. Reeve.

From Angelina he had heard twice during his absence. Her letters
were filled with fervent love, and his replies were equally warm, if not
equally sincere.

He met Angelina soon after his return, and found her the same
ardent, warm-hearted creature, full of raptures and tender feelings.

On one occasion, when seated with Angelina in an embowered
shade, Burr drew a New York paper from his pocket, and pointed out
an amusing article for her to read. It related to a tory who had been
tarred and feathered in an Eastern state.

After reading the piece, Angelina continued to look over the sheet,
and presently asked her lover if he believed that the suicides generally
attributed to religious fanaticism were bona fide cases of the kind supposed.

"Why not?" said Burr; "you know my opinion of religious sectarians.
But why do you ask?"

"Because, here is a case." And Angelina read aloud as follows:

"Yesterday evening, a young lady laboring under religious
melancholy—as it is supposed—threw herself from the end of Rosevelt
wharf into the river, for the purpose of committing suicide. She was
fortunately discovered by watchman Brown, who happened to be near
the spot at the time, who gave the alarm, and she was rescued from
drowning, and conveyed to her home at No.—First street."

Burr remained silent so long that Angelina looked at him. His face
was pale as death. The house mentioned was that of Mrs. Keating.

"You are ill!" cried the young girl.

"I do not feel very well," replied Burr. "I will go home. I shall be
better in the morning."

During his few moments of silence, Burr had arranged his plan. He
set off for New York on the following day.

There was near the corner of Pump (now Canal) and Second (now
Forsyth) streets, a druggist store, kept by a physician named Waterman,
with whom Burr had formed an acquaintance while at college.

Waterman was a young man of twenty-seven years, six feet high, and well proportioned; a noble-hearted, generous fellow, and a great admirer of the fair sex.

Burr went directly to the shop of Waterman, and found him alone.

After shaking hands, and some wise remarks about the weather, Burr said suddenly:

"Waterman, you ought to take a wife."

"I will reply to you in the words of another," said the other, laughing. "Whose wife shall I take?"

"The wife of a fine fellow named Keating," answered Burr.

"Indeed! and suppose that Mr. Keating objects to the arrangement?"

"That he will not be likely to do," returned Burr, "as he lies some six or eight feet below the surface of the ground."

"Dead! then his wife is a widow, you know. Well, Burr, you must acknowledge that it is not pleasant to have your wife's former husband thrown in your teeth upon every trivial occasion."

"Fear not. She won't do it. I'll guarantee that you'll be the gainer, both in practice and in the enjoyment of life."

"Hum!"

"Fact!"

"Then marry her yourself."

"Our ages do not suit. Nay, I am in earnest. You can have no objection to see her."

"Not the least."

"Then put on your hat."

"And leave my boy to eat up the liquorice?"

"What's the use of keeping a boy if you cannot leave your shop?"

"I set him to work with the pestle and mortar."

"Where is the drawer in which your liquorice is kept?"

"Here."

Burr wrote on a strip of paper the word Poison, in large letters, and stuck it on the front of the box.

"Can your boy read?"

"Yes."

"Then call him. Your liquorice is safe. Put on your hat, and come and see a woman who is sweeter and far more tempting than your liquorice."

"Bah! no one shall choose a wife for me."

But Burr could perceive that Waterman's curiosity was aroused, and that he placed more faith in his judgment than he was willing to confess.

Waterman went with Burr to the widow's house in First street, and the young doctor and Mrs. Keating were pleased with each other's appearance at first sight.

Mrs. Keating was very sad, it is true, but Waterman was a merry wight, and we are pleased with our opposites. The mournful tones of the fair penitent struck an answering chord in the heart of Waterman, and he was in love with her before he left the house.

Burr, with his deep penetration into human nature, had forseen this. He knew that the widow had been in love with him. She had been affected by his supposed condition, and he had carried her by a coup de main; but Waterman she really loved.

Burr went home, and left the fire which he had kindled to burn brighter and brighter until the question should be popped.

Waterman became a frequent visitor at the house of the lovely widow, and forgot to renew the scare-crow poster on his liquorice; so that the box rapidly approached a state of emptiness.

The widow was gradually beguiled of her sorrows by the tender assiduities of Waterman, whom she loved with all the fervor of her ardent nature; but a shade of deep despondency would occasionally cross her features; especially when her lover extolled her moral qualities. Finally she grew so melancholly, or, rather these moments of despondency occurred so often, that Waterman gently entreated her to make known to him what afflicted her so deeply.

She then confessed to him her fault—told him all that had occurred between herself and Burr—and, with sobs and tears, protested her utter unworthiness to be the wife of so honorable a man as Waterman.

Waterman fixed his eyes intently upon the lady all the time that she was speaking, and when she told all, he arose slowly to his feet, turned on his heel, and left the house without uttering a word.

That was a dreadful moment for the poor widow. To have lost for ever the one whom she loved to distraction was quite enough—but to have incurred his contempt also—that he should leave her without even a word of commisseration—that he should have cast her off like some abominable thing, that he would not touch for fear of pollution!

But while she is wringing her hands in agony, and almost cursing the watchman who saved her from the overwhelming waters, a step is heard in the entry—the door opens, and Waterman enters; but he is not alone. A grave personage, in a large hat, black coat and breeches, black stockings, and neat white neckcloth, with black silk gloves on his hands, follows her lover into the room.

It is a minister of the Gospel. What can be his errand there?

The lady looked wildly, first at the stranger, then at Waterman.

"This, I presume, is the bride," said the black-coated man.

"Yes," cried Waterman, in a full, sonorous voice, hearty as his own true soul.

Quicker than lightning, the enraptured young woman darted into the embrace of her lover, threw her arms convulsively around his neck, kissed him a dozen times on brow, lips, and cheek, and called him her angel, her preserver, and everything else that could express the most heart felt gratitude and adoration.

The ceremony was performed. The amiable widow embraced a noble and devoted husband, and Waterman took to his heart the sweetest angel that ever wore that blessed garment called a petticoat!

Burr was invited to the wedding supper, but with excellent taste he did not respond to the invitation. He never intruded upon the domicile of his friend. Some five years afterwards, Burr encountered, in the northern part of New York, a manly, robust figure, with large whiskers and bushy hair, who regarded the former a few moments attentively, and then rushed forward, seized his hand, and shook it most cordially.

Burr looked at him with his penetrating gaze, and cried:

"Waterman!"

"The same," was the answer. "Burr, I am bound to you for ever! I owe you a debt of everlasting gratitude."

"How?"

"You have given me for a wife the most blessed woman—"

"What!" cried Burr. "Five years after marriage!"

"Yes, fifty, if you like. She is the most noble-hearted, angelic creature—the most devoted, affectionate, constant woman—the best wife that man was ever blessed with."

"Bravo!" exclaimed Burr; "but how do you get on, my dear fellow?"

"First-rate. My business went right up after my marriage, and I am now the owner of a whole block of houses in New York, and the father of four bouncing, beautiful babies, of whom I can speak in the highest terms, for they resemble their mother in their features and disposition."

"Rascal that I am," said Burr to himself, "this one good deed of mine will be a noble off-set to a thousand wicked ones!"

VIII

Burr in the Camp—An Intrigue in Charlestown.— The Betrayed Wife

The intimacy between Burr and Angelina Dudley appears to have continued till he joined the army, in 1775, at Cambridge.

It does not appear that they ever met afterwards. Indeed, not long after their separation, Angelina was married to a British officer of wealth, who took her to England, introduced her at court, and from that time we lose the trace of her.

Burr was not well satisfied with his fellow-soldiers of the American camp. He found that discipline was relaxed, and card-playing was far more attractive than military tactics, to the majority of the patriots.

Our hero remained at Cambridge some two months, during which time he made his mark among the ladies, after his peculiar fashion.

Crossing over to the adjacent town of Charlestown, with a couple of his brother-officers, on one Sunday afternoon, Burr saw at a window a young lady of considerable beauty, who regarded him with attention.

She lived in what is called Main street, not far from the square on which the market and town-hall are built. Although his two companions were taller than himself, and might have passed for men of commanding forms and imposing aspect, yet the lady appeared to be more struck with the appearance of Burr than with either of the others.

This was of course, gratifying to the young soldier, who appears to have been remarkably vain of the admiration of the other sex. While his two friends were enjoying themselves at a hotel, he went out and made some inquiries respecting the occupant of the house which contained the young lady. He soon found that it was the dwelling of a Dr. W—, a man of considerable eminence in the town.

"Pray, sir who is this Dr. W—?" inquired Burr. "Is he a single man?"

"No, sir; he married Miss P—, of Concord," was the reply; "the prettiest girl in that place and the reigning belle."

"Belles are sometimes wanting in devotion to one man," said he, carelessly. "Having been admired and praised by many, they miss the incense of flattery—"

"Very true," replied his informant quickly, "and in this case, it was only after the repeated and earnest entreaties of her lover that she yielded her assent to the marriage. Some thought he would go mad if she did not accept him."

"A man does wrong to appeal to a young lady's pity," said Burr, "when he has reason to believe that she would not prefer him if left to her own proper judgment."

"Yes, sir, and when he does get her by appealing to her pity, he ought, at least, to treat her well."

"What, sir! do you mean to say that he does not treat her well?"

"He has been married but six months," was the reply, "and there are strange stories about him already."

"Of what?"

"You may guess."

"That he keeps a mistress, perhaps."

The other smiled, and said:

"He goes into New Hampshire once in a while."

"Are there many pretty girls in New Hampshire?" inquired Burr.

"Yes, sir; many a fair neck and bosom, with fair hair, and rounded forms—a plenty of them, sir."

"You say the wife is beautiful?"

"Beautiful, sir, but dissatisfied. Having yielded up her liberty to the prayers and entreaties of a man who seemed to love her to madness, it is natural that she should feel unhappy when he has proved, by his conduct, that he was governed by a mere whim of the moment."

Burr had, indeed, observed something in the air of the young lady that warranted him in believing every word that his informant had communicated.

Acting as if he had never seen her, Burr obtained an accurate description of her personal appearance. It was certainly the same woman whom he had seen at the window.

"Does he often leave town for New Hampshire?" asked Burr.

"Yes; he is gone there even now."

Burr said to himself:

"It is best to make hay while the sun shines. And when evening arrived, he contrived to separate from his two friends, as if by accident, and rapping at the door of Dr. W—, asked for the lady of the house.

He was requested to walk in, and the start which Mrs. W— gave when she first beheld his countenance by the light of the lamp, convinced him that she had been impressed by his appearance when she saw him in the street.

"My apology, madam, for intruding upon you this evening," said Burr, "is the fact that I am just from the colony of New Hampshire, and have been hunting for you all the afternoon."

"From New Hampshire, sir!" cried the lady, seeming puzzled at this announcement.

"You know that the Doctor is there, madam?"

"The Doctor, sir! But what doctor do you allude to?"

"Dr. W—, of course."

"Dr. W—, my husband!" exclaimed she in evident astonishment.

Burr discovered that circumstances had favored him. He had supposed that she knew the doctor was gone to New Hampshire, though she was ignorant of his errand thither.

"He is certainly in New Hampshire, madam, for I saw him there two days ago, and he sent a message by me to you."

"What was it, sir? It doubtless explains why he altered his original intention, which was to go into Connecticut."

"I beg pardon," said Burr; "such was not the nature of his communication. He wished me to say, that, owing to unexpected circumstances, he should not return under two weeks."

"You surprise me, sir. Did he not say why he went to New Hampshire?"

Burr bit his lip, as if mortified at having revealed a fact which the doctor wished to conceal.

"He did say something about Connecticut, and now I recollect, madam, that—that—bit I fear that I have distressed you."

The young wife remained silent, but looked pale and trembled.

"What his business is with Miss Johnson," continued Burr, "I do not know, but—"

"With whom, sir?"

"Miss Johnson, madam. You have doubtless heard of Miss Johnson?"

"Not I. Did he tell you that he should call on a lady of that name?"

"Oh, no. I thought you knew that, as a matter of course. I am not acquainted with the young lady, but report speaks of her as being very handsome."

"You learned—"

"I learned from a gentleman in Concord, New Hampshire, that Doctor W— frequently visited a Miss Johnson, who resides near his house. But, you seem affected, madam. Perhaps I ought to have left it to your husband to explain the matter."

"I have long suspected something wrong, sir, and now I see it all."

"I don't say that. The young lady is probably some patient of his; or, indeed, she may be a relative. You have no cause to—"

"Oh! no, sir. Your interpretation is quite too charitable. Why should he tell me that his frequent absences are caused by business in Connecticut?"

"That does look—unaccountable," said Burr, hesitating. "Yet there are so many ways that—at least, he might have some cogent reasons for not telling you where he was going."

"Yes, sir, but he does tell me where he is going, and tells me falsely."

"It is impossible, madam, for any one who has seen his lady, to believe that Dr. W—, can be attracted elsewhere."

"I believe, sir, by your manner, that you know even more than you have told me."

Burr started, but remained silent; still he looked as if he was surprised that she should have so truly interpreted his manner.

"Come, sir, let me hear the worst at once."

"It is not my province, and very unpleasant to my feelings." returned the young soldier, looking at Mrs. W—, with an expression of deep sympathy on his countenance; "it is not my habit to foment misunderstandings between a husband and his wife, but rather to allay them."

"Nay, sir, the whole truth—whatever it be—cannot equal the dark suspicions which are engendered by this tormenting suspence."

"Madam, I am sorry that I was made the messenger on this painful occasion; but an intimate friend of your husband has told me that he said you never loved him—that you only married him for the sake of attaining to a social position—that you were afraid of dying an old maid."

"My husband said that! What, after all that had passed—after he had—but no matter." And the poor woman's cheeks were, at once, deluged with a flood of tears.

"Madam—dear madam," cried Burr, soothingly, but his sympathy availed little. The thought that a man for whom she had sacrificed herself, and to whose prayers and tears she had yielded rather than to her own feelings and preferences, should so misrepresent her conduct and character, was quite to much; and she continued to weep bitterly.

Burr then began to speak of himself, and of his intention to accompany Col. Arnold on an expedition to Canada. This awakened the interest of the lady, who asked if it was not exceedingly dangerous.

"That is its principal recommendation to a soldier, madam."

"But you are so young! Pray, sir, may I make so bold as to ask whether your parents are living."

"They died while I was a mere child; but I have other relatives. I have a sister."

"Does she know that you intend setting out on this dangerous enterprise."

"She does, and though feeling all the anxiety which does so much honor to the tender heart of a woman, is yet patriot enough to surrender me to my country."

Mrs. W— sighed. In his conversation, Burr had contrived to render himself extremely interesting. His youthful appearance was calculated to set the mind of the lady at rest in regard to any danger to her honor that might attend their private consultation, while his glowing countenance, his gallant air and determined heroism, united to that magnetic power which dwelt in his beaming black eyes, occasioned her feelings that she would have been very unwilling to confess to the world. It grew late, but the young lady heeded it not. The hours passed like minutes, for her spirit was enthralled by Burr's conversation, which from sympathy took the tone of love, and yet so gradual was the change that she could not have told when or how it was affected.

We have said that the lady's husband never possessed her love; but, after the disclosures made by our hero, she did not even yield the false husband her respect.

The time was propitious for the object which Burr had in view, and he seized the opportunity like a Napoleon on the battle field.

Nearer and nearer he drew his chair to the lady, and finally threw himself on his knees before her, and poured out a rhapsody in terms admirably suited to such an occasion.

But this startled her from her dulcet dream, and she beheld the abyss that yawned before her. A less intrepid wooer would have shrunk from her awakened indignation; but Burr only felt himself at the Bridge of Lodi, and was equally to the emergency. He now, for the first time, laid his hand on the lady, and hugged her to his bosom, kissing her with such earnestness as to smother the shriek which quivered on her lips. Another moment, and she lay prone upon the sofa, with her dress over her face. So quick were the movements of Burr, that the young wife felt the ecstatic thrill before she could collect her scattered senses, and then it was to late. Such sweet joy rushed through her heart and titilated her woman-hood, that all sense of duty or fear of discovery was swallowed up in the present enjoyment.

Again and again did Burr apply himself to the task of consoling the neglected wife, and day dawned before he left the entranced beauty to her own meditations.

She watched him from the window, as he walked rapidly up the street, and wondered how one so youthful should have learned so much of the female heart, and should be so able to satisfy its desires when the raging fire of passion had once been kindled.

IX

An Awkward Predicament.—The Mechanic's Wife and
Aaron Burr.—The Mother-in-Law and Her Daughter

On the succeeding Sunday night, Burr repaired to the house of
Mrs. W—, and having ascertained that the husband had not yet
returned, he entered the apartment were he had left the lady of the
house.

She was there, and welcomed Burr with much warmth; but she was
the prey to remorse. She declared that the misconduct of the doctor did
not excuse her dereliction from the path of duty. Not caring to multiply
words, Burr proceeded to administer consolation in his usual style, and
the lady soon forgot her troubles in Elysium.

Burr urged the propriety of retiring to bed, where they could pursue
their bent to more advantage. She resisted awhile, but finally yielded
her assent.

The pretty woman retired first, and having undressed, blew out the
light, and got in between the sheets.

Burr went up in the dark, and placing his clothes on a chair near the
door, where he could easily find them, turned down the coverlet, and
rushed into the arms of Mrs. W—, who received him nothing loth.

They were soon buried together in untold bliss. This was repeated
several times, and it was not far from midnight, when Burr felt a cold
human hand laid upon his neck. He knew by the feeling that it was not
the little soft hand of his companion, who, indeed lay panting and half-
fainting by his side, unequal to any physical exertion.

It might be a servant, a somnambulist, or a robber: but it might
also be the husband of the lady, and now he remembered that, in their
heedlessness of all worldly matters, they had stolen off to bed without
locking the front door.

"Clarissa!" said a well known voice, "is this you?"

"My God! how you scared me!" cried the startled wife; "why did you
not bring a light?"

"But Clarissa, it is not your head that my hand rests upon. You are
not on this side. You are over yonder—"

"Has that dog—as sure as the world, that Newfoundland dog of
Mr. Fosdick's has crept in. Get out! oh! get out! cried she, kicking and

pushing Burr, who took the hint, and tumbling out on the floor, ran along on all fours till he came to the door, when he snatched his clothes, and ran down the stairs.

But the husband, who had his suspicions, had thrown open the shutters—which were on the inside of the window—and saw Burr, by the bright moonlight, as he seized his wardrobe, and vanished out of the door. Accordingly he immediately gave chase; and the doctor was rather a dangerous customer, as he always traveled with pistols, and had a pair in his pockets, loaded and primed at that time.

Burr reached the hall door before the doctor had arrived at the landing of the stairs, and hastily turning the key, was about to dart down the steps, when he perceived two or three men passing near the house.

He at once perceived that a man flying in his shirt, from the house, pursued by the doctor, would compromise the reputation of Mrs. W—; and drawing back, he slammed the door violently, and turned aside into the front parlor, the door of which stood ajar.

The doctor flew down the stairs, and having heard the street door open and shut, supposed the intruder had gone out that way. He ran into the street, and hearing foot steps near the corner, drew out a pistol, and rushed up to the gentleman whom he found there.

The individual thus assailed had stopped behind some large sugar-boxes in obedience to a call of nature, and was "in the full tide of successful experiment," when the doctor seized him by the collar, dragged him out, roaring:

"Don't try to hide yourself there, you infernal scoundrel?"

"Why—why—what is the matter?" asked the other, trembling in every joint; and then seeing the pistol in the hand of the other, he bawled aloud: "Watch! watch! help! robber! robber! robber!"

Fortunately a watchman was close at hand, who came immediately up, and seized the doctor by the arm.

"How! Doctor W—!" said the officer; "what is the matter, sir?"

"This fellow, here," cried the doctor, vehemently, and shaking his victim at the same time—"I just caught in bed with my wife—"

"No, no, doctor! Impossible!"

"But I tell you that it is possible. Didn't I see him run out of the room with my own eyes. You see that he has not yet had time to button up his clothes, which he snatched from a chair as he ran out of the chamber," cried the doctor, pointing to the man's flap, which still hung down.

"No—but, Doctor W—, this gentleman is well known to me. He is the Rev. Mr. P—, of Concord."

The doctor let go of the stranger, and stared with all his eyes.

"Well, I believe you are right," said he "but where then is the man who has done this thing. He came out of the front door—"

"I guess not," interrupted the watchman. "I was opposite your house when I heard the door open and shut, but no one came out, until you made your appearance."

"Say you so? then the rascal has secreted himself in the cellar or in the back yard." And the doctor ran back to the house without stopping to apologize to the reverend gentleman whom he had shaken so violently, and frightened almost out of his senses.

When the doctor left the house, Burr justly presumed that he would soon return, and made the best use of his time. He slipped on his clothes, and had scarcely buttoned them when he heard the angry husband's footsteps on the pavement under the window. He fled to the back door, which he opened quickly and closed silently, just as his indignant pursuer entered the house. He ran through the yard to the back door of a house that abutted on the doctor's premises and plunged into the first apartment that presented itself; but not until he had bolted the door after him.

The doctor went down to the cellar with a light in one hand, and a pistol in the other, which gave Burr ample time to say to the lady of the house which he entered, and whom he found still up and engaged in sewing.

"Don't be alarmed, madam. I am an American officer, pursued by three virulent tories, who have sworn to take my life, as I officiated at the tarring and feathering of one of their number."

The lady at once banished her fears, and replied:

"Then, sir, you shall be protected as far as it can be done. We are no friends to the British here. They burned my father's house over his head, and we only ask that Washington and his army may drive the whole swarm of red coats out of the country."

"I am an officer of the army at Cambridge," was the brief reply of Burr, for the doctor had found nothing in the cellar, and was now thundering at the back door of the house which our hero had entered.

"There they are now!" exclaimed the lady.

"You may as well go to the door, and tell the rascals that I am not here; but ask them what they want first."

The lady ran out to the door, and cried:

"Who is there, and what do you want?"

"I am your neighbor, Dr. W—," was the reply; "I want a rascal who is concealed somewhere in the neighborhood, and I thought he might have entered your house."

"Merciful heaven!" said the woman to herself, "is the doctor among the tories? I'll never employ him in my family again as long as I live!" Then she added aloud:

"You see the door is fastened. How could he have got in here?"

"Very well, Mrs. G—, I beg your pardon. He has probably got over the fence and escaped."

Mrs. G—entered the room with a pleased smile on her countenance, but soon said:

"Do tell me, sir, if our neighbor, the doctor, is an enemy to his country too?"

"Certainly. One of the very worst kind, as he conceals his principals, and only avows himself when he gets a chance to strike down a patriot."

"The snake in the grass!" exclaimed Mrs. G—, bitterly. "Well, who can we trust in these days—unless, indeed they are soldiers like yourself, actually engaged in fighting for liberty."

"True, madam, but—"

Burr was interrupted by the husband of the lady, who called from an upper chamber:

"Come, my dear, are you not coming to bed yet?"

It was evident that the man had just been awakened by the doctor's noise at the door, or rather he was only half awake, to judge by the tone in which he spoke.

"I cannot come yet, Silas, for I must finish this jacket before I sleep, as Mrs. Pease wants it for her son tomorrow at farthest."

The good man seemed to have dropped immediately to sleep again.

"You must know," said the woman, in a low voice, to Burr, "that my husband is afraid to commit himself, as his employer is a bitter tory, though he don't make a noise about it, and if it was known that we hid you from your enemies, Silas would be turned off at once, and we find it hard enough now to make the two ends meet."

"Worthy woman," said Burr, who was immediately melted with compassion; "accept this, and rely upon more in a day or two."

Burr handed her a gold piece of some value, which she took, with a blush on her cheek, which made her really look handsome.

She was so young that Burr had, at first mistaken her for a girl. She was scarcely of the middling height, plump, and very lively, with small feet and hands, black eyes and hair, vermilion lips, and a good, wholesome complexion.

This young woman had been very merry in company before her marriage, and loved the beaux very much; yet it was not known that she had ever lost her virtue. She had married a man because she was in great haste to gratify those feelings which nature has bestowed upon the most chaste and prudent of her sex. But she had not made a choice commensurate with her necessities. Her husband married because he wanted to settle in life, and have a woman to take care of his wardrobe and cook his victuals. He never was much pleased with the society of the fair sex, and Mrs. G— soon discovered that his embraces were cold, and that her glowing charms inspired little admiration in her lawful companion. She should have married a very different man.

Burr detected the young creature in casting several glances at his person, and some of those glances were so directed as to give pretty sure evidence that his sex was not the least circumstance which recommended him to her protection and sympathy.

Burr commenced a conversation, and spoke alike with eyes and tongue. The result was, that before he had been in the house an hour, the amorous young woman was enjoying inexpressible transports, such as she had never before imagined. In her ecstacy, she overset a chair, which, in its turn, knocked down a Dutch oven, that came rattling upon the stone hearth.

The noise aroused the husband, who cried:

"Come, my dear, do tell me if you are going to set up all night?"

The entranced creature did not reply, in the hope that he would fall asleep again; but he immediately called out again:

"Sally! Sally! have you got asleep?"

"No-o-o!" cried she, wriggling with intense pleasure in the arms of Burr. "No-o-o! I am no-not-aslee-slee-aslee-ee-eep. Not aslee-slee-oh! oh! slee-eep."

"Why don't you come to bed?" demanded he, aloud.

"Yes-yes-I'm com-um-um-um-ing-ing com-ing-ing-ing."

"What's the matter with you?" cried the man, now fairly awake.

"The cat has bit my finger, and it hurts so-o-o-o!"

"It sounds as if you were going into a fit," cried he; "like the highsterics!"

"Oh, yes, it fee-fee-ee-eels so-o-o-o!"

Just as the husband bounded out of bed, the young woman had experienced the final keen agony of joy, and by the time the good man had put on his breeches, and began to descend the stairs, she had sufficiently recovered her senses to cry—"Scat! scat! scat!" and to chase Burr with the broom, who, imitating the squall of a cat, ran to the front door, which the young woman opened hastily, and Burr darted into the street.

When Mrs. G— returned to the room, her husband was there.

"Now," said he, "don't let that cat ever come into the house again: if you do, I will tie a brick to her neck, and sink her in the river. Mark my words. But let us see where she bit you?"

"Oh! it was nothing—only I felt vexed at first."

"No, you don't speak the truth, for you are writhing and twisting your stern one way and another as if you felt dreadfully, just as one does when they can't stand still for the pain they are suffering."

"Well, well, look at it then," cried she, having bitten her finger slightly, just so as to start the blood.

"Vengeance!" exclaimed the husband. "The cretur has left the marks of her teeth, for I can see 'em as plain as day!"

"Well, the brute creature don't know any better, Silas, so let it pass."

Silas looked at his wife, whose cheerful manner was more like that of a person who was filled with the sweetest delights, than one who had received a bite from a cat, and he said to himself:

"The woman is very happy with me; that is certain. It takes me to render a woman happy."

In the last adventure, Burr had certainly conferred great pleasure upon a young and amorous woman, besides aiding her in a pecuniary manner, and these reflections were agreeable to him. He believed that no harm would result to any one concerned, as the husband would never know what had taken place.

In the other case, he feared that harm would ensue. There was something in the look and manner of Mrs. W— that enlisted his sympathy. He was certain that she had married from purely disinterested motives, and that he for whom she had sacrificed all, had flung her to the wind, and received another in her place. Yet why should he have done this? Burr had ample proof that her limbs were elegantly formed, and other more secret charms were ravishingly delightful, and that in the sexual act itself, she was eager and fervent.

As his person was unknown to Dr. W—, Burr visited the neighborhood, and finally became acquainted with the following facts: Dr. W— did not sleep at home that night. Weary with travel, and none the less so for having exhausted his physical powers with the New Hampshire beauty, he repaired to a public house, rather than to go through a scene with his wife before he had recruited his energies.

In the morning he went home full of wrath and vengeance. He found the servant, but not his wife. She had prudently gone to her mother's house in Lexington. Not doubting that his wife had gone to the maternal mansion, the doctor put his horse to the chaise, and drove out to the village.

His wife was not visible, but the old lady presented herself. She was a square-built dame, with embrowned cheeks, and large gray eyes, with sound teeth, and hair scarcely streaked with gray. One could not look upon that form and countenance without feeling that the old lady was equal to any emergency.

"Is my wife here?" asked Dr. W—, with the air of a deeply-injured man.

"Well, she is, sir," was the reply of the good lady, who smoothed down her apron, and shook her exhuberant locks, like a general placing his troops in order for battle.

"Then, madam, I must see her"

"Must is for the king, sir."

"In short, madam, she has defiled my bed, I caught a man in bed with her last night."

The old lady drew a long breath. She had supposed that the parties had only quarreled, and that her daughter had fled before the storm.

The charge was a serious one; but like Bunyan's Great-heart, who was at first knocked down upon his knees by the giant's club, she soon recovered herself, though her countenance remained quite pale, and she said:

"Do you say this of your own knowledge, sir?"

"I tell you that I saw the man in bed my wife, your daughter," cried the doctor, bravely, perceiving the impression he had made.

The old lady sighed, passed her hand over her brow, and said:

"Pray, sir, where were you, and what were you adoin' on when my darter was left with another man, as you say?"

"What was I doing?" said the doctor, eyeing the woman keenly, "why—why, I was out of town, as I am often obliged to be."

"You are obleeged to be, you say, sir, and what obleeges you to go and leave your wife every few weeks in these troublesome times, when the rig'lars is goin' about like a roarin' lion a seekin' somebody to devour?"

"We will not discuss that point, madam; but I will appeal to any respectable physician—"

"Well, if you won't 'scuss that p'int, sir, nyther will I s'cuss the tother p'int, and you may go back as empty as you came."

"I claim my wife, madam, and insist upon seeing her."

"That can't come to no good, sir. If your wife has done what you say, you don't want nothin' of her, without it is to abuse her for what she's done; and thar's a doubt in my mind whether you've got a right to do that."

"And why not? Don't she deserve it?"

"I'll tell you what, sir, If my darter really is guilty of what you say, then I tell you that every one says you are guilty of doin' the same thing, and that you have done it a great deal more than she ever did, and it's my opinion that 'what's sauce for the goose is sauce for the gander,' and so you know my mind, and that's all I've got to say."

The old lady then retired to the kitchen to prepare dinner, and Doctor W— went out and walked alone in the woods. He could not but confess to himself that he had neglected his wife, and that he had been very intimate with a widow in New Hampshire, though not with a Miss Johnson, as falsely stated by Burr.

Another thing: the doctor had foolishly supposed that his wife had married him because she could not get any body else, and the fact that another man had sought her in his absence served to remind him of the attractions which she really possessed, and which had once inspired him with the most vehement desire.

Added to all this, the New Hampshire widow had become exorbitant in her demands upon his purse, and had grown petulent and even scornful because he did not supply her large demands.

"If even Clarissa has been false in my absence," said he, "what may not the other be? Doubtless she expends the large sums which she extorts from me on other lovers—perhaps upon some low country clowns, who, wanting funds of their own, make her pay for their vulgar embraces instead of paying her."

This thought decided him, and he returned to the mansion.

Although she had carried it so bravely in the presence of the doctor, like a poor old hen defending her one chicken from a hawk, yet the mother of Clarissa had been dreadfully pained by the discovery of her daughter's error. She sprinkled flour upon the asparagus, and pepper on the pudding; she made several other mistakes, and when she perceived them, she threw herself on a stool in one corner, and said:

"There! I shall never be myself again," and covering her face with her hands, she wept aloud, to the great wonder of the maid, who asked her if the rig'lars were coming back.

In the next moment the good lady was told that the doctor wanted her in the parlor. She dried her eyes and went to him.

"Tell Clarissa to come," said he, in a voice that the old lady understood, and went to her daughter who was, after some persuasion, induced to go down to her husband.

"Clarissa," he said, taking her hand, "we have both done wrong. Nothing is left but for us to forgive each other. But one man knew of your misconduct, and I have bribed him to silence. We may yet be happy."

Clarissa hid her face in his bosom, and the old lady kissed her son-in-law on the forehead and blessed him, while her tears flowed like rain.

This couple were, indeed, happy, for Doctor W— never afterwards alluded to the unfortunate subject, and ceased paying his visits to New Hampshire.

Clarissa, who had never given her husband credit for generosity, now loved and respected him. What more was needed?

X

Burr Carries a Message to Gen. Montgomery.—His Adventurers at a Convent.—The Beautiful Nun

Aaron Burr confessed to an intimate friend, at Staten Island, a few days before his decease, that he had never embarked on any dangerous expedition, nor approached any event which was destined to make a great change in his fortunes, without being strongly impressed with the remembrance of ADELAIDE KING, the unhappy maiden who had yielded up her virtue to his youthful doings, with whom he had commenced that career of intrigue and seduction, which carried sorrow and ruin into the bosoms of so many families.

As the time drew near, when he should set out, with Col. Benedict Arnold, for Canada, the image of Adelaide King frequently rose before his mind's eye; but it was not altogether a sad impression. There was a sort of pensive pleasure attending her imaginary presence, as if she loved him still, and was waving him on to glory and renown.

It was late in September, in the year 1775, when Arnold embarked at Newburyport with his troops, and Aaron Burr was with them.

We need not detail all the particulars of their journey, which was partly by water and partly by land. They passed through the wilderness, encountering steep mountains, tangled swamps, and morasses; and were exposed to a variety of hardships, such as were calculated to appal the stoutest hearts.

When the troops reached Chandiere Pond, Col. Arnold wanted a brave and trusty messenger, by whom he could send a verbal message to George Montgomery. He had an opportunity of witnessing the gallant bearing, the intelligence and activity of Burr, and fixed upon him as the bearer of the message.

Burr knew that the French Catholics were discontented with the government, and for that reason, he adopted a disguise that would afford him access to that portion of the community. In short, he assumed the disguise of a young Catholic priest, and thus accutred, he set out upon his perilous adventure.

Burr applied to one of the reverend gentlemen whom he counterfeited and revealed his true character and intentions. The priest entered into the spirit of it, and supplied our hero with a guide and a cabriolet.

In this way, Burr traveled from one religious family to another. When he had arrived within a day's journey of Trois Rivieres, he put up at an old convent, the venerable building of which was almost a ruin, so that he could not avoid being brought into direct contact with the nuns.

The Lady Superior informed him that a partition wall had lately given way, and was so much cracked and fallen, that she had it taken down, for fear it should tumble of itself and hurt some of the young ladies.

Although it was an object to keep the nuns from the presence of man, and they were, therefore, prevented from seeing travelers who passed by, yet, if a man was to be entertained at the house, there was no alternative. He must be visible to the inmates; and this state of things would continue until repairs could be made in the building.

Young Burr gallantly replied that he was thankful to the accident which had revealed to him so much beauty and innocence, adding, as he saw the Lady Superior turn an anxious eye upon the listening and gratified nuns: "I mean, madam, the beauty of innocence—that beauty which virtue and devotion never fail to confer upon the 'human face divine,' whether it belongs to your sex or to ours."

The Lady rewarded the speaker with a calm smile of approval.

"For instance," continued Burr, "what is more beautiful than the face of Madonna and yet it is a beauty which is calculated to excite none, but the most holy emotions in the soul!"

By this time, the Lady Superior was calmed with the pious sentiments of our hero, but the nuns, who had listened to every word, showed plainly by their looks that they gave him little credit for sanctity and asceticism. From the time that Burr entered the building, the nuns had fixed their eyes upon him with that eager and intense gaze, common to young ladies who have been immuned in their season of love, and sedulously prevented from seeing man.

To them there is an overwhelming attraction in the masculine countenance, in the tones, bearing, and in every peculiarity of the proscribed sex. These girls feasted their eyes with the handsome young soldier, as if they would gladly devour him, like so many wolves, if they could obtain permission to do.

Whatever he did, whichever way he turned, their eyes clung to him, and every motion was watched as closely as the naturalist watches the movements and peculiar developments of some strange animal, which he has seen for the first time, and which he has procured from some adventurous traveler, at an enormous expense.

While she was absent, making some arrangements for his accommodation, in an upper chamber, Burr turned his eyes full upon the nuns, who were congregated at the distance of some ten or twelve feet from the spot in which the lady superior had placed him.

We have spoken of the singular magnetic influence of our hero's eyes, and the perturbation which it caused in the bosoms of the fair sex. When young Burr turned his full black eyes upon the nuns, and regarded them with passionate admiration—they exhibited much emotion. There was a fluttering among them, as if a bomb-shell had burst in their midst. They blushed, turned pale, their lips quivered, they looked at each other, and, finally, at Burr again, reminding one of the passage in Solomon's Song:

"Thou hast ravished me with one of thy eyes!"

These girls were very generally interesting, and one of them was eminently handsome. Her large blue eyes swam with tenderness, and her abundant hair was of the finest and most glossy brown; her features were regular, and her mouth peculiarly beautiful. Her form was voluptuous, and her general appearance bewitching in the extreme.

This was sister Catharine; her real name was Antoinette Mortier. She had been bewitched by the attentions of a handsome French officer, who left her for another, but without having received any favors from her, if we except a few amorous kisses.

She was disconsolate when her lover deserted her, and, in a fit of melancholy, threw herself into a convent. Two years had passed, and it is probable that the Frenchman was forgotten, for she fastened her blue eyes upon the countenance of young Burr, with an earnestness that told how capable she was of feeling the most passionate desire for the opposite sex.

Now that the lady superior was absent, Burr looked very tenderly at the amorous and beautiful nun, and she scarcely turned away her eyes from his, so thrilled was she by the magnetic influence, while her passions, long controlled, were threatening to consume her.

All this, Burr saw, in an instant. He knew that Sister Catharine was dying for the embrace of a man, and his natural benevolence prompted him to undertake her cure, if such a thing were possible.

But how could this be effected? The nuns were under the strict supervision of the lady superior, and how could so great a sacrilege be committed without discovery, and the mortal offence would be given to the church authorities, and to the priests who encouraged the expedition, and upon whom Burr depended for protection?

Many men would have been discouraged, by those prudent reflections, from making any attempt to comfort and console this amorous young lady. But Burr was too mindful of the welfare of the sex to let any consideration intimidate him.

He believed it impossible for these nuns to continue always within doors, and he did not doubt that, when darkness veiled all outward objects, they were in the habit of taking the air.

When, therefore, he retired to his room, Burr did not undress, but sat watching at a window which looked out upon a paved court; and he observed that he could easily get from his window upon the roof of a sort of moss-grown portico which jutted out from the rear of the main building. From thence, the descent to the ground was easy.

Scarcely had he taken his place at the window, before he saw some person moving out from the little covered passage-way, and slowly walking along the pavement. Burr stooped down so as to be invisible from the court, for he had heard a low sigh breathed by the unknown, and something told him that it was Sister Catharine, the beautiful nun.

She spoke, though in a low tone. He held his breath to catch the accents which came from those lovely lips:

"For two long—long years," said she, "have I endured this, and what do I gain by thus denying myself the indulgence that nature loudly calls for? I feel that something calamitous must ensue if this is continued much longer. Nature is isolated. Madness itself cannot be far off! Oh! rash and foolish girl that I was! and now I have seen one of that sex forbidden to us—ay, forbidden even to look upon those masculine countenance, so winning—so seductive—so lovely—oh! my heart do not burst quite—"

There she threw herself on the pavement, and sobbed in an agony of grief and despair, which none can conceive of but those who, like her, look forward to life-long misery.

This was quite enough for Burr. He slid down from the window upon the portico, and then sprang to the ground as lightly as an antelope. The melancholy girl heard him as his feet struck the pavement, and looked around.

She recognized him at once as the strange visitor, with the wonderful eyes. He rushed towards her.

"Back! back to your room!" cried she, placing her white hands against his forehead and shoulder. "Back, on your life! Discovery would be destruction to us both!"

"Beautiful, angelic creature! my love forbids it. I cannot live without one kiss from those heavenly lips of yours. Suffer me to take but one kiss."

"Oh! my God!" cried she, waving her hands, "what shall I do?"

"Nay, is not the good lady asleep?" asked he, clasping her around the waist, and kissing her violently.

She answered not, though she tried to do so, but her voice was choked by her emotions, by her heart swelling with love and passion that quite mastered her. She sank into his arms, sighing deeply.

Burr drew her into the portico, where was an old settee; and having hastily thrown up her dress, he passed his hand along those plump limbs those round thighs, as smooth as polished marble, and then he touched the most sacred spot of all, which betrayed the amorous fire which consumed her.

The beautiful nun now struggled to prevent an exposure, which too plainly told how much she was under the influence of burning desire, but soon all thoughts of shame were lost in joys unutterable!

Even the pang of losing her virginity was unheeded by the frenzied girl; for so keen was her desire, that the pain, itself, seemed to be delightful to her, knowing, as she did, what caused the momentary sufferings. The plump and rounded "mons veneris" being vigorously pressed by the ardent youth, in the act of coition, shot forth its jets, causing the nun such sweet throes of pleasure that she writhed, sighed, and could scarcely prevent herself from screaming. The seat of pleasure itself, influenced as it was by long-suppressed desire, now rubbed by the instrument of manhood, burned with such intensity of joy, that her motions became convulsive. She clasped Burr with arms and legs. She turned her limbs about him—her eyes rolled with maddening delight—she caught his lips between hers and sucked them till they were bloodless, and we will not repeat the exclamations, the phases of wild and inflamed affection which she lavished upon him, as her bounding heart swelled with gratitude to the handsome youth, who was filling her whole being with the sweetest raptures that imagination can depict.

When the climax arrived, the belly and thighs of the youth were bathed with what seemed to be burning lava, so ardent was this amorous maid, so hot was her blood after two years of hopeless repining at her virgin state.

Burr then regained his feet, when the nun sprang up and threw herself upon his breast, clutching him like a cat, so fearful was she of losing the author of her sweet transports. Burr then rained kisses on her mouth, neck, and bosom.

"Oh!" said she, "my heart! Oh! my soul! Oh! my God! to think what I lose by remaining in this cursed convent! Oh! my dearest, most blessed Man! Oh! Sweet Man! Oh! blessed Man! Oh! heavenly Man! Let me eat a piece of you! You have so thrilled me—so delighted me! so sweetened me—come—come," and she drew consoler down upon her bosom.

Burr then gave her the second part of the same performance, in which she was, if possible, more enraptured than the first time. So bereft of all prudence, of reason, was the thrilled and delighted girl that, when the final keene throe of pleasure arrived, she threw back her head convulsively, and gave one loud, wild scream expressive of her intolerable joys.

Burr gave up all for lost; but no one stirred. Accustomed as they were to all sorts of noises, from wild beast and straggling Indians, the inmates of the convent, when startled from their dreams, by any strange cry, only crossed themselves, repeated a pater noster, and went to sleep again.

After listening some minutes, and perceiving that no one came. Burr proposed to the loving beauty that she should go up with him into his room, and after a moment's reflection, she acceded to the proposal. What could she refuse him at that moment? She would cheerfully have laid down her life to give him one moment's gratification.

With little difficulty, Burr assisted the nun to gain the top of the portico. He then lifted her into the window of his chamber.

During the removal of the beautiful girl to his chamber, Burr's passion was enkindled to the last degree. Lifting her about in his arms, and thus becoming cognizant of the rounded plumpness of her form, the full and protuberant posteriors, the voluminous thighs, and the fleshy calf, he felt a trembling eagerness to deposite her on his couch, and a dread of interruption, not from any fear of consequences, but because he could not think with any patience of losing the prize so opportunely placed within his reach.

Very soon, however, they were in the room, and Burr having closely drawn the curtains, relighted his lamp. Then he looked upon the sweet morsel of heavenly food which lay panting upon his bed, impatient to be pressed once more in his arms.

The delightful young creature looked more beautiful than when he saw her first.

She had experienced pleasure since then; and the rich color—the flush of her cheeks, the softened expression of her loving eyes, the humid redness of the lips slightly ajar, the bosom, all conspired to render an object of adoration, of sincere worship.

Burr could not resist the temptation to survey those beauties which were hidden by the gloomy drapery of superstition. He raised her dress above her knees, and as the light fell full upon them, and revealed their luxurious fullness, he ardently kissed the glowing flesh, and then higher he ventured, lifting the drapery till it revealed all. He kissed the white round belly, sweeter than the honey of Hybea, and then remarked the full voluminous thighs, their glossy smoothness, and the exquisitely beautiful, pouting, little, heavily-thatched paradise which lay between them. What he did then we will not pretend to know; but he caused the nun to wonder and sigh, and finally to put down her hand and press them against the back of his head, as if she loved the action greatly.

Burr examined and admired all her beauties, from the swelling loins to the well-turned ankle and little feet. Then again, they met in the ardent encounters of Venus, and the night wore fast away.

At length, the lovely nun informed Burr that she must leave him, as day-light would reveal her absence from her dormitory.

They sat together upon the edge of the bed. She announced that the time had come for leaving him—yes, HIM from whom she had tasted those long-desired joys, which now she must probably forego for ever!

Burr knew what was the subject of her thoughts, by the earnest, sad, and despairing manner in which she gazed upon him. He afterwards confessed that that was the most unhappy moment of his life.

To leave that beautiful young creature whose sweetness he had tasted till his enraptured sense could endure no more—that loving girl who adored him with her whole mind and heart—to leave her a victim to pangs which now would be more cruel than ever, rent his heart with anguish.

"I shall think of you when far away," said Burr, pressing her to his heart, and giving her one long ardent kiss.

"But I shall see you no more," said she, in that low, hopeless tone of forced resignation, which is more agonizing to the hearer than the most tumultuous grief.

"We may meet again, and I will make it a point to visit the convent at some future time," returned Burr, and with this assurance, he aided the half-fainting girl down into the court, where they took a mournful leave of each other, and repaired to their respective couches.

XI

DEATH OF GEN. MONTGOMERY.—BURR'S RETURN HOME.—
MISS MARGARET MONCREIFFE, THE YOUNG ENGLISH GIRL

Captain Burr soon exchanged love for war, and instead of warm kisses from amorous lasses, he received the welcome of grape-shot and musket balls.

Burr was equally at home in either station. The wars of Venus, or those of Mars, always found him ready and effective.

The attack on Quebec was made on the morning of December 31st, 1775, before daylight. The snow was falling fast at the time. Burr and other officers had endeavored to dissuade General Montgomery from leading in the attack; but the gallant Irishman persisted in his first resolve to take up his station in the front of the battle.

While they were advancing, a piece of artillery in the British battery went of accidently. A fortunate accident it was for the British, but a most deplorable one for us. The brave Montgomery, and every other person in the front, excepting Captain Burr and a French guide, were killed. When Montgomery received his death wound, he was within a few feet of Captain Burr, who was his aid-de-camp at the time.

General Arnold now assumed the command of the army, and young Burr was called upon to perform the duties of brigade major.

In the spring of 1776, Burr left the army under Arnold, and started for home.

When our hero arrived at Albany, he received a message from General Washington, that it would be agreeable to him if he would visit New York. Burr set out accordingly, and reached the city of New York on the 20th of May, 1776. Washington invited him to join his family at head-quarters, till he received an appointment. This was at Richmond Hill.

Burr was dissatisfied, and wrote to John Hancock, The President of Congress, who offered him the appointment of aid-de-camp to Major-General Putnam. Burr accepted it, and removed from the head-quarters of the Commander-in-Chief to those of Major-General Putnam, which were also in New York, in the large brick house at the corner of Broadway and the Battery.

Although Burr was now much engaged with his military duties, yet it would appear that he had some leisure to attend to the fair sex also.

One morning, rising rather early, he saw from his chamber window, which looked out upon the garden, an unexpected apparition, standing in the midst of a grass-plot, edge round with a box.

This was a young lady, not quite fourteen years of age, whose form and features were apparently English, and of extraordinary beauty.

The rich black eyes, red cheeks, exquisitely beautiful mouth, roundness of the face, and general wholesomeness of aspect, were certainly English. The form of the shoulders, plumpness of the bust, and vigor of her movements, with a certain indescribable fullness of nature and self-possession, left little doubt in the mind of Burr that she was from the land of George III, with whom he and his compatriots were at war. He also observed that she was richly attired in a robe of cherry-colored silk, trimmed with lace en point d'Angleterre; a gold band encircled her forehead, and about her neck was a beautiful necklace, composed of a triple row of pearls, and a magnificent opal.

But withal, she wore these things with such a perfect grace and nonchalance, that one would scarcely observe her dress, while her beauty would have stirred the blood beneath the ribs of an anchorite. Burr thought he had never seen so glorious a neck. Every motion had a soul in it; every look, every step, every turn of her head, was perfectly natural and unaffected, yet had a charm so winning and unique that Burr stood looking upon the lovely vision perfectly entranced, and forgetful of the fact that she might, by just elevating her eyes, detect the bold gaze of her stealthy admirer.

This did, indeed, happen. She looked up and saw Burr, upon whose countenance was to plainly visible the interest which she had awakened in his breast.

He withdrew immediately, but not until the young lady had caught the expression of his magnificent black eyes.

At the breakfast table, Burr met the young creature again, who sat opposite to him, and upon Burr it devolved to help her to whatever she wanted, and to pay those little attentions which characterize well-bred society.

He now perceived that the young lady was accustomed to polished manners, and her replies were delivered with a grace and self-possession peculiarly her own, while her repartees and bon mots both surprised and delighted him. In short, she was somewhat eccentric, and expressed her opinions with a freedom and enthusiasm not usual in one who had scarcely attained her fourteenth year.

But her expressive countenance, and the charm which she threw around everything that she said, divested her out-spoken sincerity of every appearance of impropriety; and as soon as the family arose from table, Burr begged Mrs. Putnam to tell him who the young lady was with whom he had had the honor of taking breakfast that morning.

The good lady told him that the young girl was a daughter of Major Moncrieffe, of the British army. She had resided in Elizabethtown, New Jersey, while her father was with Lord Percy, on Staten Island.

The best way to account for her residence with General Putnam, is to give her own words, as they appeared in Memoirs written by herself some time afterwards. She says:

"Thus destitute of friends, I wrote to General Putnam, who instantly answered my letter by a very kind invitation to his house, assuring me that he respected my father, and was only his enemy in the field of battle; but that in private life, he himself, or any part of his family, might always command his services."

"On the next day, he sent Colonel Webb one of his aid-de-camps, to conduct me to New York. When I arrived in the Broadway (a street so called), where General Putnam resided, I was received with great tenderness by Mrs. Putnam and her daughters, and on the following day I was introduced by them to General and Mrs. Washington, who likewise made it their study to show me every mark of regard; but I seldom was allowed to be alone, although, sometimes, indeed, I found an opportunity to escape to the gallery on the top of the house, where my chief delight was to view, with a telescope, our fleet and army at Staten Island."

"My amusements were few; the good Mrs. Putnam employed me and her daughters continually to spin flax for shirts for the American soldiers; indolence being totally discouraged; and I likewise worked some for General Putnam, who, though not an accomplished muscadin, like our dilletantis of St. James' street, was certainly one of the best characters in the world; his heart being composed of those noble materials which equally command respect and admiration."

Such was Miss Margret Moncrieffe, daughter of Major Moncrieffe, who had placed herself under the protection of the noble-hearted Putnam.

She had been in the family but three days, when Burr, having gone to the house-top to make some observations on the enemy, heard another individual approaching. He took little heed of this, untill the appearance on the platform of Miss Moncrieffe caused him to start with both surprise and pleasure.

Seeing Burr with the telescope, she merely bowed, and was about to retire, when Burr immediately tendered her the instrument, saying that he should esteem it a happy epoch in his life that he was able to afford any pleasure to so excellent and charming a young lady as Miss Moncrieffe.

"Oh! by no means, sir," returned she, blushing; "my observations have already made me acquainted with the value which my dear General Putnam places upon the services of Major Burr, and the curiosity of a girl like myself should not be permitted to—"

"Nay, I was only gratifying my own curiosity at present; and the curiosity of a lady is legitimate, and has claims upon us for its gratification."

"Still, sir, I shall be best satisfied to retire," said she, casting down her eyes, and turning to descend the steps.

"If my request will avail nothing," returned Burr, "I can give you Scripture for pursuing a contrary course to that which you propose."

"Indeed, sir!" cried she all alive to hear how Scripture could apply to her movements.

"We are admonished," said Burr, "in this wise: 'Let him that is on the house-top not come down.'"

"Well, we are upon the house-top, certainly," said Miss Moncrieffe, with a light, ringing laugh, and looking at Burr with some attention; "but, sir, I can think of another Scripture, that two shall be together, and that 'one shall be taken and the other left.' I fear that yon, sir, must be the party that is left, especially as your text says, 'Let Him (not Her) that is upon the house-top not come down.'"

Burr replied:

"I am unhappy that in a Scripture controversy Miss Moncrieffe should have the advantage of me, since it deprives me of her company, but I am about to retire, and since you insist that, 'one shall be left,' let it be yourself, since I know that you would not have come here if you did not wish to remain awhile, and the slightest wish of Miss Moncrieffe will always have the force, with me, of an order from head-quarters."

Burr then descended so quickly that Miss Moncrieffe found herself alone ere she was aware of it.

When Burr went to his military duties, after the above-mentioned interview with the charming English girl, he first asked himself whether

Miss Moncrieffe had really wished to avoid being alone with him. What would have been more natural, thought he, than for a young lady to accept of the attentions of one of the opposite sex, who could prepare the telescope for her, point out and name the various locations and objects at which she desired to look; and, in short, pay those ordinary attentions which common gallantry requires?

"Why, then," said he, to himself, "should she be so fastidious? Why not remain with me a few moments? Certainly she is not bashful; she can be free enough when the rest of the family are present. Indeed, perhaps, the attentions of the general have turned her little head, and she thinks that any thing below a general officer ought not to meddle with her. Nay, she has seen Washington; perhaps that he has said something in her presence, that was calculated to lower me in her estimation. If I thought so—but pshaw! Why indulge suspicion, when there is not a shadow of proof? If she is a haughty aristocrat, it is enough. Perhaps that I have now hit the right nail on the head. I will be ruled accordingly. Ah! my fine bird in fine feathers, you shall see that an American officer does not twice lower his crest to the minions of royalty."

With this resolve in his head, and a flame of admiration for the young girl in his heart, Burr went to his duties.

Though he did not neglect the tasks which devolved upon him, Burr continued to think of the young girl, and longed for the dinner-hour, that he might show her, by the cold formality of his attentions, that he thought no more about her.

"I will, as if by accident, speak highly of some fictitious young lady, whom I will pretend to have seen in the course of the morning," said he to himself, "and that will account for my coldness towards her. She will perceive that I am no provincial booby, to imagine there is no other pretty woman in the world, but the maid of the mill to which he carries his bag of corn."

With these feelings and sentiments, Burr entered the dining-hall. The place of Miss Moncrieffe at the table had been changed; she was no longer his vis-a-vis. Opposite to him sat the General's eldest daughter.

Burr could scarcely conceal his feelings. He now felt certain that his interpretation of the young girl's conduct was the true one—that Miss Moncrieffe was too arrogant to receive his attentions, and had altered her position at the table on purpose to avoid them.

He did not know how to act: he mechanically waited upon Miss Putnam, who, holding Burr in high esteem, accepted his kindness with the most evident delight, and endeavored to make herself as agreeable as possible.

Then it came into Burr's mind that he would treat Miss Putnam with marked politeness, and he became so engaged in his manner towards her, that she, once or twice, looked up with evident surprise.

At length our hero glanced towards the place where Miss Moncrieffe was seated, for the purpose of discovering whether she noticed his demeanor, for he had wanted to impress her with the idea that it was not on account of any peculiar admiration for her that he had been so attentive when the care of her devolved upon him, but that it was only his custom, when dealing with any one of her sex.

He looked, therefore, at the young English lady, and was surprised to perceive that her eyes were fixed upon his countenance, with an expression of mournful anxiety, and also, that she ate but little, and scarcely replied to the officer who addressed her.

Burr was sorely puzzled. If she really regarded him with respect, why had she changed her place?

When dinner was concluded, Burr met the beautiful English girl in a passage, who stopped him, and reaching out a penknife, said:

"This is, I think, the property of Major Burr, left on the house-top this morning, when he so kindly relinquished the telescope for a silly foreigner, who had not the good manners to thank him a he descended. That silly foreigner has punished herself by sitting in another place at table, and thus denying herself those pleasing attentions, from a brave and noble-minded young officer, which she has justly forfeited by her conduct towards him."

"Ah! but, my dear Miss Moncrieffe, it is not yourself whom you punish," cried Burr, seizing her hand hastily; "it is that young officer, whose merits your generous nature prompts you to estimate far above their value. You punish HIM, Miss Moncrieffe, when you place it out of his power to be near you—to attend to your wishes."

"Say you so? Oh! then, that alters the case," replied she, deeply blushing, and then added with a smile:

"Nothing would have given me greater happiness than to have kept company with Major Burr on top of the house, but he must remember that I came up last—I felt as if it might appear that I knew you were there."

Burr felt the force of this apology, and wondered that he had not given the circumstances of their meeting due weight before. Miss

Moncrieffe had been surprised at finding Burr on the house-top, and had been fearful that her conduct would be misconstrued.

"You speak truly," said Burr; "there might be cases in which suspicious persons would entertain such a notion: but no one who knew Miss Moncrieffe would dare to do so, and certainly never to express the unworthy thought"; and Burr laid his hand upon his sword in a threatening manner.

Miss Moncrieffe was evidently pleased with Burr's mode of treating the subject, and, with downcast eye, she passed on to the inner room.

It might have been supposed by some, if they had witnessed this interview, that Burr would have felt pretty sure of winning the heart of Miss Moncrieffe, and receiving favors in consequence of it. But our hero was not so sanguine. The frankness of Miss Moncrieffe under the circumstance, the self-sacrifice which she had made in confessing her supposed fault, argued, in the mind of Burr, against such flattering hopes; for here seemed to be displayed a coolness of judgment, and heroic perseverance of duty, which he had not looked for in one so young, and so enthusiastic in her admiration of liberty, and of those who were fighting to obtain it.

The deportment of the English beauty, immediately subsequent to that time, strengthened Burr in his opinion of her character and conduct.

Miss Moncrieffe took her former place at the table, but she accepted the attentions of Burr, with such acknowledgements as any well-bred young lady would have felt warranted in returning to a meritorious officer who resided in the family of her protector, while her conversation remained as lively and piquant as ever, and she took her full share in the general topic of remark, whenever it was one with which she was acquainted.

This state of things remained several days, and Burr had began to believe that Miss Moncrieffe would be careful not to meet him again in the passage, when, one day, that he chanced to be standing near her, he heard a low sigh. At the same moment, he turned, his eyes fell on the young lady, and she colored deeply.

The next time that Miss Moncrieffe went to the top of the house, Burr followed her. He pretended to be taken by surprise when he saw her at the telescope; but approached her with these words:

"Miss Moncrieffe is surveying her good friends at Staten Island. I fear that we colonists are but dull companions for one who has been accustomed to European habits, and to the various amusements which are so rife in her native land. Perhaps that she sighs for scenes far away, and would gladly return to them."

"On the contrary, sir, I love America dearly; and its people, struggling for freedom, are certainly, at this moment, the most interesting of any on the face of the globe."

"You do us honor, and from the lips of beauty, what so cordial to the soldier's heart as such commendation."

Burr then proceeded to draw Miss Moncrieffe's attention to several interesting views, both seeming pleased with each other.

"See yon green slope," said Burr, "on the far side of the Hudson, where lately the Indian gamboled, ignorant of the very existence of civilization, till our fathers came and robbed him of his home. How happy might two loving hearts be in that bosky solitude, roving among the sunny glades, and listening to the music of ten thousand birds, their couch the heather and their canopy the green leaves of the forest!"

Burr fixed his eyes boldly on those of the English girl, as he uttered these words, and his soul beaming through them, seemed to indicate that if she were his companion, he could happily spend his life amid the wild flowers and the purling brook of that charming landscape.

Miss Moncrieffe was silent, but she looked at Burr, and then cast down her eyes, as if inviting him to go on.

As Burr waited for a reply, she murmured:

"Yes, it would be a perfect paradise."

Burr then took her hand, which was not withdrawn, and said:

"With such a one as yourself, for instance."

Miss Moncrieffe interrupted him by a light laugh, and said:

"Me!" cried she, "why Mrs. Putnam considers me a mere child!"

"You are not a child in intelligence," returned Burr, "nor in deportment."

"Yet I don't think I can go over there with you at present, as I have not spun my share today; and that reminds me that I have loitered long enough on the house-top."

The young girl then descended with Burr, who was satisfied with his morning's work, and believed that he had paved the way to a better acquaintance with Miss Moncrieffe.

On the ensuing Sunday, Burr proposed a ride in the environs of the city, to which Miss Moncrieffe acceded all the more readily that her life was somewhat monotonous at the general's house, and any thing like variety was attractive to her.

Burr procured a horse and chaise, and they set out. Our hero drove slowly out of town to a shady lane, since known as "Love Lane," and there fastened the horse to a tree, when both descended, for the purpose of getting a few flowers.

"Mrs. Putnam is so kind," said the young lady, "and I know that a few of these would please her much."

"Yes," said the young soldier, "and now we can commence our life, in the way we talked about, when we surveyed the pleasant landscape at the other side of the river."

The English beauty was, at that moment, very busy in gathering flowers, and did not raise her head till the blush had passed away, which had suffused her cheek at hearing words which might well be interpreted as a profession of love, or something of the kind.

Burr assisted her in her task till he had found a beautiful lily, which he said she should place in her breast, as it would well become her; then he officiously undertook to pin it there, pressing her bosom rather more than was absolutely necessary in performing the task.

Miss Moncrieffe did not say that she was ticklish in that place, but she certainly acted as if she was susceptible of some sort of feeling, while Burr, with affected clumsiness, was fumbling round her bosom.

Burr was very attentive, very polite, and assisted the young lady with an empressement which certainly was not without its effect.

Her words became very soft; she looked into his eyes from time to time, and read there what seemed to be the most devoted affection and the most exalted admiration.

The afternoon waned, and the trees cast their shadows long and round upon the grass. It was a delightful solitude. The murmuring of the streams was heard, the birds flitted among the branches over their heads, and no human footsteps ventured near them. They sat enjoying the cool breeze that rustled among the leaves, upon a green bank, and talked freely of the various subjects that arose, one after another, in the fertile mind of Burr.

At length, his arm stole around her waist; she sighed, he kissed her on the lips, and her head dropped on his shoulder. Burr gently laid her back upon the grass, and she was helpless in his hands. He was surprised that she offered no resistance to his attempts upon her virginity.

The truth is, that her heart had long ago been won, though Burr knew it not, and her feelings had, that afternoon, been wrought up to the highest pitch. Therefore she sank passive upon the grass, and Burr threw up her dress, revealing all her budding charms to his enraptured gaze. He had not expected to find so much development. Her limbs were unusually plump and robust, and all things invited to those transports which they soon enjoyed to fruition.

It was now that the young girl betrayed the love which she had felt for Burr, almost from the first moment she saw him. She clung to him, kissed him, and wound herself about him with a perfect frenzy, and told him over and over again that her heart was entirely his, and that she would go with him through fire and water, death, or dishonor.

It is needless to say that Burr made her thoroughly acquainted with pleasures of which she had before no conception, and indeed he found her sufficiently able to perform her part in the encounters of Venus.

At length, the lateness of the hour warned them that their return should be no longer delayed, lest suspicion of the truth should visit the minds of the good people at home.

After one last embrace, in which their very souls seemed to rush from their bodies, they returned to the chaise, and set out for the residence of General Putnam.

On the way home, Burr was surprised at the depth of love and tenderness in so young a heart as that of Miss Moncrieffe. She frankly told him everything how she had been struck by his appearance—"pierced to the heart," she termed it—the first time that she saw him; how she, at first strove to conquer her passion; but found it impossible; and that, at all their subsequent meetings, she had had much ado to keep from rushing into his arms and avowing her love.

Never had Burr listened to such a rhapsody as she poured forth, smothering him, ever and anon, with the most ardent kisses.

But, however enraptured the English beauty had been by the embraces of Burr, and the enjoyments of those new and unimagined transports that she had found in his arms, she possessed sufficient judgment to behave with perfect decorum when she appeared again in the presence of the family.

She dwelt at large upon the beautiful scenery she had found in the rural sections, and all her talk was about flowers, birds, trees, and landscapes, as if she had thought of nothing else since she had been gone.

Yet Mrs. Putnam did perceive something unusual in her looks; but if she suspected the truth, she did not make her suspicions manifest.

For three or four days, Burr had very little opportunity for conversing with Miss Moncrieffe. His time was much employed in his military duties, while Mrs. Putnam, on the other hand, was hurried with work, and Miss Moncrieffe found her task at the spinning-wheel increased.

The glances which the fair girl now began to cast at Burr convinced him that she was growing impatient of this state of things, and that she longed to be alone with him once more.

He intended, therefore, to propose another ride on the coming Sunday, and while he lay awake at night, thinking upon the subject, he imagined that he heard a light footfall in the entry. As the next chamber was occupied by his general and lady, this caused him to start up and listen, for the thought, at first, struck him that some mischief might be intended towards the gallant old chief.

He then heard the handle of he lock jar slightly, as if some one had laid his hand upon it. It was, perhaps, some intruder, who had mistaken his room for that of the general's.

He arose softly, and felt for his pistols; but at that moment, a low, soft voice came to his ear, like that of a woman, and he knew by whom his privacy had been invaded. He flew to the key, turned the bolt softly, and Miss Moncrieffe stood before him.

"Margaret, my love!"

"Aaron, dear!" was the response, and Miss Moncrieffe glided into his arms.

"How could you come to me and escape detection?" whispered he.

"The sentinel at the landing of the stairs was leaning on his musket fast asleep."

"Aha! I'll see to that tomorrow."

"No, you must not, for it was my fault. I mixed him the nicest little glass of punch that you ever tasted."

"You mixed it!"

"Yes; I gave him a night-cap which would send a devout anchorite to the land of dreams, when watching at the Holy Sepulchre at Jerusalem."

"Treason!" cried Burr, kissing her little pouting mouth. "Oh! let women alone for concocting mischief—"

"And sleeping potions," said she, archly. Burr shook his head with an air of mock reproof, but in reality felt concerned at this proof of Miss Moncrieffe's adventurous spirit. What might she not attempt next?

Burr removed from the shoulders of the young girl a cloak which she had thrown over her when she left her chamber, and she stood before him in her shift. He then took her in his arms, and laid her in his bed, quickly springing in after her.

This was a luxury indeed. For several hours they took their fill of love, revelling in such delights as only stolen pleasures yield, when attended with a perfect sense of security.

Miss Moncrieffe never forgot the joys of that night, to the latest day of her existence. She was enraptured with the performances of her lover, who enjoyed free access to all her youthful charms, and thrilled her with his caresses and embraces.

When the time came to part, she flung herself on the breast of the young soldier, and expressed a regret that she could not grow there forever. But the gray dawn had already made its appearance, and go she must; so—

> *"Vowing oft to meet again,*
> *They tore themselves asunder."*

Burr dressed himself, and went out first to reconnoitre. He found the sentinel at his post, and attentive to his duty. He dispatched him on some trifling errand, and then saw Margaret to her sleeping apartment. He then threw himself down, and enjoyed a refreshing sleep.

XII

MISS MONCRIEFFE'S NIGHT ADVENTURE.—HER REMOVAL
TO KINGSBRIDGE AT THE INSTANCE OF BURR.—HER RETURN
TO HER FATHER, AND SUBSEQUENT COURSE.—BATTLE OF LONG
ISLAND.—RETREAT FROM NEW YORK.—LOVE ADVENTURES
ON THE BANKS OF THE HUDSON

When Sunday came, the lovers rode out again, and once more they were in Paradise. On the very next night, Miss Moncrieffe came to the chamber of the young soldier, at the great risk of discovery, for she passed the sentinel while on duty, and if he had chosen to mention the fact, her reputation would have been compromised.

Burr felt that she had acted imprudently, but he took "the good the gods provided him," and she spent a glorious night. But she became incautious even in the day time, and addressed Burr at the table in such gentle and affectionate accents, that even General Putnam observed it, and looked up in some surprise. Her visits to Burr's chamber became frequent, and, in short, she evinced a recklessness of consequence which warned him that the time had come for them to separate.

Burr took an early opportunity to confer with General Putnam in regard to Miss Moncrieffe, and represented to him that she was well calculated for a spy; that notwithstanding her youth, she was very intelligent and observing; that she listened intently to all that was said in regard to the present difficulties between Great Britain and the Colonies and asked many questions about the plans, opinions, and intentions of the commander-in-chief. Such a person, he suggested, ought not to be permitted to remain at head-quarters, or in the family of Gen. Putnam.

Putnam spoke to Washington on the subject, and he suggested that Miss Moncrieffe should be sent to Kingsbridge, where General Mifflin commanded.

After a brief stay at Kingsbridge, leave was granted for Miss Moncrieffe to depart to Staten Island. An American officer took her in charge, and they set out for the British head-quarters in a boat.

When they had come within a short distance of the English fleet, they were met by a boat from the latter, and the British officer commanding gave them to understand that they could go no farther; that he would take charge of the young lady and convey her in safety to her father, who was six or eight miles in the country with Lord Percy. In her Memoirs, she adds:

"I then entered the British barge, and bidding an eternal farewell to my dear American friends, turned my back on liberty."

The Memoirs also contain the following rhapsody, in relation to a young American officer, meaning Aaron Burr:

"May these pages one day meet the eye of him who subdued my virgin heart. * * * * To him I plighted my virgin vow. * * * With this conqueror of my soul, how happy should I now have been! What storms and tempests should I have avoided (at least I am pleased to think so) if I had been allowed to follow the bent of my inclinations. Ten thousand times happier should I have been with him in the wildest desert of our native country, the woods affording us our only shelter, and their fruits our only repast, than under the canopy of costly state, with all the refinements of courts, with the royal warrior (the Duke of York), who would have fain proved himself the conqueror of France. My conqueror was engaged in another cause; he was ambitious to obtain other laurels. He was a colonel in the American army, and high in the estimation of his country. His victories were never accompanied with one gloomy, relenting thought. They shone as bright as the cause which achieved them."

After Miss Moncrieffe's return to her father, she married, and took her husband's name, which was Coghlan. Her conduct towards her husband proved but too plainly that her heart was elsewhere. She became widely known as a gay woman, and the name of Margaret Coghlan was frequently mentioned in the court and fashionable circles of Great Britain and France. Lords, dukes, and members of Parliament sought her acquaintance, and she was alternately reveling in wealth and sunken in poverty. But through all the changes, adventures, and vicissitudes of her varied and inconstant life, she appears to have entertained for Burr, "the conqueror of her soul," the most ardent respect and admiration.

Soon after the departure of Miss Moncrieffe, Burr was called into active service.

Putnam was on Long Island with Major Burr as his aid-de-camp, when the British landed near Utrecht and Gravesend, on the southwest end of the island. This was on the 22d of August 1776.

The battle was fought on the 27th, in which the Americans lost, in killed and wounded, and prisoners, one thousand men. The loss of the British was little more than a third of that number.

The result is not surprising when we consider the superiority of the enemy, who had a force of twenty thousand men—the Americans but twelve hundred.

The Americans were driven within the works which they had thrown up, and before the British had commenced their attack, a retreat was ordered.

A thick fog probably saved our army from destruction. Under cover of the heavy mist, the whole army, nine thousand in number, with all the field artillery, ordnance, and other paraphernalia, were safely landed in New York.

Burr was appointed a lieutenant-colonel in the Continental army in June, 1777, and on the 14th of July, he was sent by Gen. Putnam to Norwich and Fairfield, there to watch the movements of the enemy, or any of their fleets.

On the 26th of July, Burr was officially notified that he was appointed lieutenant-colonel of Col. Malcolm's regiment, at that time stationed at Ramapo or the Clove in Orange county, New York. Burr was at that time twenty-one years of age, and appeared even younger than that.

Malcolm was a merchant of New York City, and had been appointed to office because he was a man of influence; but he relinquished the command to Burr, saying: "You shall have all the honor of disciplining and fighting the regiment, while I will be its father."

He then retired with his family about twenty miles distant, and never commanded his regiment in battle, during the war, although it was frequently engaged. That duty was performed by Burr.

While Burr's regiment was at Clove, the British came out of the city of New York, on the West side of the Hudson, about 2,000 strong, to plunder and devastate the country. Burr heard of the enemy at the distance of thirty miles, and was in their camp with his 300 men before morning, capturing and destroying their picket-guards and sentinels, which struck such consternation into their ranks that they fled with precipitation, leaving behind them their plunder and a part of their stores.

On the next day, Col. Burr received orders to join, without delay, the main army, then in Pennsylvania.

One little event occurred, during Burr's stay with his regiment at Clove, which, though it has no connection with the war, we hope our readers will pardon us for inserting.

Burr was walking out, one Sunday afternoon, near a wood on the banks of the Hudson, pondering on matters connected with his military duties, when he met, in an unfrequented place, a young lass some sixteen or seventeen years of age.

Her neat pink-spotted calico frock was tucked up around her waist, to avoid the briars, discovering a snow-white petticoat, and very neat feet and ankles. She wore a broad brimmed straw hat, tied with a wide green ribbon, and was otherwise dressed in the neat attire of a villager of the middling class.

The form of the young woman was admirable, and her countenance pleasing. She had large blue eyes of a peculiarly sweet expression, cheeks delicately tinged with red, and though the lips were full, the mouth was handsomely formed.

The young woman, perceiving that Burr was an officer of the army made him a low courtesy. He bowed and bade her "good afternoon," to which she responded as is usual in such cases.

"Pray my dear miss," said Burr, "have you seen anything of a hound during your walk?"

"I have not, sir," was the reply; "I met the large dog, near the corner of the wood, which belongs to the store, but he is not a hound, sir."

"I am sorry for having troubled you. You were in haste to get on, I believe, as I observed that you walked with great speed, and thought to myself that few young ladies could have got over the ground so quickly."

"Oh! I was only coming from a visit to my aunt, sir. But there are so many cow-boys and tories, that I was a little afraid."

The young officer laid his hand upon his sword, and said rather pompously, to produce an effect:

"Let me catch any of the rascals lurking about here, or following on your steps! It is the duty of a soldier to place his body as a wall of defence between danger and the fair sex: and where beauty like yours is periled—"

"Oh, sir!" cried she, blushing deeply, while admiration sparkled in her eyes.

Burr retarded their progress as much as possible by stopping occasionally to remark something on the Hudson, or in the wood, and then he made some observation to his companion, in which he contrived to throw in a spice of flattery.

Then he assisted the pretty girl to get upon a rock, to see some object he had pointed out to her, and while doing so, he would suffer her bosom to come in contact with himself, and so gradual was his progress, and so naturally did it all appear, that he was soon walking

ANONYMOUS

with his arm around the waist of his companion. Then he pressed her form rather abruptly, which caused her to turn her face towards him rather reproachfully.

"Forgive me," said he; "but who could be so near these captivating graces without desiring to make the contact closer? Do you not know that you are very beautiful?"

"I do not know that I was every called so," said she looking down.

"It is then because you have not been with good judges. It is not every one who is capable of appreciating true beauty. We have many young ladies among us who are good looking, who have good hair, good teeth, or a handsome mouth and chin; but when all the graces have met in one, oh! there we look and worship!"

Burr did not say that in the young girl before him all the graces had met, but he looked it, and she felt that it was to her he alluded when he spoke of a perfectly beautiful young lady.

They passed on, Burr having taken her arm, which trembled very perceptibly. He lifted her over a brook, and perceived plain evidences of emotion.

By this time it was dusk, and a beautiful day in September. They were on a grassy path, with flowing banks on either side, Burr in the act of extolling the charms of the pretty rustic, at the same time gave her several kisses on the neck and bosom. This alarmed her some, but he followed up the first offence closely by another, till, finally, she sank into his arms. He then drew her to a little covert, and forced her down on the heather, her strugglings becoming weaker and weaker. In another moment he had revealed all her charms—the taper legs, the round white thighs, and the beauteous spot which promised joys and raptures which cannot be described.

For a moment she was aroused to a sense of her condition, and repulsed the bold invader of her sanctum sanctorum; but he smothered her with kisses, and with an "oh!" and an "oh! dear!" she acknowledged that the Rubicon had been passed.

Untold pleasures followed. Streams of joy titillated and delighted her young and ardent womanhood, until rapture followed rapture in such quick succession that her sweet blue eyes rolled wildly in their sockets; she quivered from head to foot, she threw her legs over her lover, and exhibited all the proofs of pleasure and transport of which woman is capable on this side of the grave.

When the climax arrived, the sensation was so new and startling, that she uttered a scream, but there was nobody to hear it except Burr, and he was too experienced a veteran in the wars of Venus not to understand its meaning.

When the deed had been done, and the young girl realized the fact that she was no longer a maid, she looked first at Burr, and then on every side, as if a doubt of her personal identity had seized upon her. The idea of ever surrendering up her virginity to any man but her husband had probably never entered her head before. After thus testifying her wonder, remorse, and even dispair a moment, she sank panting at the feet of Burr.

He raised her up, and supported her in his arms. She looked in his face a moment, as if to chide, but changed her mind and let her head fall upon his shoulder, when she burst into loud weeping.

He tried to console her, by saying that no one would ever know what she had done; that many respectable young women even had children privately, and that their reputations never suffered in consequence of their false step; but he found that nothing else would answer the purpose, so he again had recourse to the never-failing cure all—in such cases

He caressed her anew, and soon aroused her passion again, when he found her even more excitable than on the first occasion. She experienced the keenest pleasure; and when all was over, she lavished the most affectionate words upon him. This led to a third and forth performance, by which time the young girl declared that she could delay her return home no longer, and that somebody would be sent by her friends if she did not go home immediately.

Accordingly, they set out, conversing very tenderly with each other, and the young girl giving her promise that she would meet Burr again.

The young soldier was somewhat surprised to find, on reaching the home of his companion, that she resided in a very large mansion, and that her father was a man of wealth and influence among the inhabitants of that part of the country.

Burr met this young girl several times afterwards, and found her pleased with his attentions until he left that post, and went to join the main army.

Col. Burr was sent for by Washington, to join the main army with his regiment, because the British army under General Howe had crossed the Schuylkill several miles below the place where the Americans were encamped.

Shortly after Burr's arrival with his regiment at head quarters, the army went into winter quarters at Valley Forge.

While at Valley Forge, Burr attended strictly to his military duties, but found some time to attend to the fair sex, who, like wild flowers entwining the rugged rocks, beautify and consecrate the hardships and dangers of a soldier's life.

XIII

BURR AT WESTCHESTER.—STORMING OF THE BLOCK HOUSE.—
ADVENTURE WITH CAROLINE DRAKE, OF PLEASANT VALLEY

After the retreat of Sir Henry Clinton from Philadelphia, through New Jersey, during which there was some fighting, in which Burr did good service, our hero took command of the lines in Westchester.

This was considered a station of some distinction. Burr immediately set about reforming abuses, for there was exhibited, all along the frontier, previous to the arrival of Burr, one continued scene of plunder, and sometimes of murder.

The following extract of a letter addressed by Samuel Young, of Mount Pleasant, to Commander Valentine Morris, under date of 25th January, 1814, will give some idea of Burr's vigilance, singular fore-sight, and power of winning the regard of those among whom his lot was cast:

"A few days after the Colonel's arrival, the house of one Gedney was plundered in the night, and the family abused and terrified. Gedney sent his son to make a representation of it to the colonel. The young man, not regarding the orders which had been issued, came to the colonel's quarters undiscovered by the sentinels, having taken a secret path through the fields for the purpose. For this violation of orders, the young man was punished. The colonel immediately took measures for the detection of the plunderers; and though they were all disguised, and wholly unknown to Gedney, yet Colonel Burr, by means which were never yet disclosed, discovered the plunderers, and had them all secured within twenty four hours. Gedney's family, on reference to his register, appeared to be tories; but Burr had promised that every quiet man should be protected.

"He caused the robbers to be conveyed to Gedney's house, under the charge of Captain Benson, there to restore the booty they had taken, to make reparation in money for such articles as were lost or damaged, and for the alarm and abuse, the amount of which the colonel assessed, to be flogged ten lashes, and to ask pardon of the old man; all which was faithfully and immediately executed.

"These measures gave general satisfaction, and the terror they inspired effectually prevented a repetition of similar depredations. From this day plundering ceased. No further instance occurred during the time of Colonel Burr's command, for it was universally believed that Colonel Burr could tell a robber by looking in his face, or that he had supernatural means of discovering crime. Indeed, I was myself inclined to these opinions. This belief was confirmed by another circumstance which had previously occurred. On the day of his arrival, after our return from visiting the posts, conversing with several of his attendants, and, among others, Lieutenant Drake, whom Burr had brought with him from his own regiment, he said: 'Drake, that post on the North river will be attacked before morning; neither officers nor men know anything of their duty; you must go and take charge of it; keep your eyes open, or you will have your throat cut.' Drake went. The post was attacked that night by a company of horse. They were repulsed with loss. Drake returned in the morning with trophies of war, and told his story. We stared, and asked one another—'How could Burr know that?' He had not then established any means of intelligence.

"The measures immediately adopted by him were such that it was impossible for the enemy to have passed their own lines without his having immediate knowledge; and it was these measures which saved Major Hull, on whom the command devolved for a short time, when the state of Colonel Burr's health compelled him to retire.

"These measures, together with the deportment of Colonel Burr, gained him the love and veneration of all devoted to the common cause, and conciliated even its bitterest foes. His habits were a subject of admiration. His diet was simple, and spare in the extreme. Seldom sleeping more than an hour at a time, and without taking off his clothes or even his boots.

"Between midnight and two o'clock in the morning, accompanied by two or three of his corps of horsemen, he visited the quarters of all his captains, and their picket guards, changing his route from time to time, to prevent notice of his approach. You may judge of the severity of this duty, when I assure you that the distance which he thus made every night must have been from sixteen to twenty-four miles; and that, with the exception of two nights only, in which he was otherwise engaged, he never omitted these excursions, even in the severest and most stormy weather; and except the short time necessarily consumed in hearing and answering complaints and petitions from persons both above and below the lines, Colonel Burr was constantly with the troops.

"He attended to the minutest article of their comfort; to their lodgings; to their diet; for those off duty he invented sports, all tending to some useful end. During two or three weeks after the colonel's arrival, we had many sharp conflicts with the robbers and horse-thieves, who were hunted down with unceasing industry. In many instances, we encountered great superiority of numbers, but always with success. Many of them were killed, and many were taken."

"Soon after Tryon's retreat, Colonel Delancey, who commanded the British refugees, in order to secure themselves against surprises, erected a block-house on a rising ground below Delancy's bridge. This Colonel Burr resolved to destroy. I was in that expedition, and recollect the circumstances.

"He procured a number of hand-grenades, also rolls of port-fire, and canteens filled with inflammable materials, with contrivances to attach them to the side of the block-house. He set out with his troops early in the evening, and arrived within a mile of the block-house by two o'clock in the morning. The colonel gave Captain Black the command of about forty volunteers, who were first to approach. Twenty of them were to carry the port-fires, etc., etc. Those who had hand-grenades had short ladders to enable them to reach the port-holes, the exact height of which Colonel Burr had ascertained. Colonel Burr gave Captain Black his instructions, in the hearing of his company, assuring him of his protection if they were attacked by superior numbers; for it was expected that the enemy, who had several thousand men at and near Kingsbridge, would endeavor to cut us off, as we were several miles below them. Burr directed those who carried the combustibles to march in front as silently as possible. That on being hailed, they were to light the hand-grenades, etc., with a slow match provided for the purpose, and throw them into the port-holes. I was one of the party that advanced. The sentinel hailed and fired. We rushed on. The first hand-grenade that was thrown in, drove the enemy from the upper story, and before they could take any measure to defend it, the block-house was on fire in several places. Some few escaped, and the rest surrendered without our having lost a single man. Though many shots were fired at us, we did not fire a gun.

"After Colonel Burr left his command, Colonel Thompson, a man of approved bravery, assumed it, and the enemy, in open day, advanced to his headquarters, took Colonel Thompson, and took or killed all his men, with the exception of about thirty.

"My father's house, with all his out-houses, were burnt. After these disasters, our troops never made an effort to protect that part of the country. The American lines were afterwards changed, and extended from Bedford to Croton Bridge, and from thence, following the course of the river, to the Hudson. All the intermediate country was abandoned and unprotected, being about twenty miles in the rear of the ground which Colonel Burr had maintained."

The above extract gives but a faint outline of Burr's services in the Revolutionary war; yet thus much it was necessary to say in order to give something like a reason for the high esteem in which he was held by the fair portion of creation.

At the time mentioned above, when Col. Burr compelled the robbers to carry back their plunder to Gedney's house, there was an acquaintance of Mrs. Gedney's, from Pleasant Valley, paying a visit to the family.

She was a wholesome country girl, without any great pretensions to beauty, by the name of Drake. But though not really handsome, she had a fine pair of black eyes, a pretty mouth, and was rather above the middling height. She was rather slender than gross in her form.

Burr perceived, while attending to his duties, that she frequently fixed her eyes upon him, and while she invariably applauded the generosity of his conduct towards the family, she thought him a very handsome young officer.

All this Burr, with his quick penetration, could read in her looks and manner. Without seeming to be impertinently curious, he discovered who she was, and that her father was a tory as well as Mr. Gedney. He kept his eye upon her, from day to day, until one afternoon when she had strayed farther than usual into the woods, he fastened his horse to a fence, and hastened to the spot where she was.

Burr affected to be very much surprised at finding her there.

"Miss Drake, I believe," said he.

"Caroline Drake, sir," said she, with a courtesy.

"A pretty name for a pretty girl," returned Burr.

She simpered and looked down.

"Miss Caroline, were you ever kissed?"

"Oh, sir! we never do such things up in Pleasant Valley.

"Not at the parties—not when you play pawns?"

Caroline did not like to say yes, or to tell a lie, so she remained silent, and looked roguish.

"I was going to say," continued the young soldier, "that if you had been kissed, you must have been told that you were very sweet, for you certainly look so."

"I never was told so, sir."

"Never was told what, Miss Caroline?" "What you said."

"But I am very desirous to find out whether you are so or not; for I feel pretty sure that you must be very sweet."

Burr then approached her, and very gently gave her a kiss on the lips

"It is as I thought," said he, "you are so very sweet, that I should be very thankful for another kiss."

She looked up, half chidingly, but with a pleased countenance, which made her sweeter than ever.

Burr ventured to press her to his heart, as he rained some dozen or two kisses on her mouth, neck, and cheeks. The latter became quite rosy, and as Burr retired a step from her, she stood before him drooping like a rose surcharged with dew, and not precisely knowing what to do under such peculiar circumstances.

He took her hand, and pressing it to his bosom, swore that she was the most lovely creature that ever wore a petticoat. She looked down to see if her petticoat was in sight below her frock, for how otherwise, thought she, should he know that I had on such a garment.

Burr then walked along with her a little ways, praising her beauty, and then, as if fired with unbounded love and admiration, seized her around the waist, and after kissing her violently, laid her down upon a mossy bank. Her feelings were awakened. She breathed heavily, her eyes were turned away from Burr, and she sighed with delight, yet struggled to free herself. Burr lifted her dress, she tried to put it down with her hand; he got his knee between hers, and taking advantage of a moment when she was overcome by his caresses, he suddenly threw her clothes over her bosom, and exposed all her charms to his observation.

Her limbs were more symmetrical than he had imagined. The calf was robust, and the thighs very full and round. Of other charms it is unnecessary to speak, except to say that they kindled the most ardent fires in his blood.

It would appear, however, that she was not quite a virgin, though by no-means, an experienced hand at this business. Burr thought she might have had a lover once, to whom she granted one or two favors, but she was very fresh and ardent.

She responded well to his passionate embrace, and they were mutually thrilled and delighted at the adventure.

This girl always entertained the highest admiration for Burr; though she afterwards married, and became the mother of twelve children.

We now approach the time when Burr retired from the arduous services of a soldier. Ill health required the sacrifice of his favorite pursuit, and his hopes of preferment, and on the 10th of March, 1779, he tendered his resignation to the Commander-in-Chief.

General Washington made the following reply:

MIDDLEBROOK, 3rd April, 1779

SIR

I have to acknowledge your favor of the 10th ultimo. Perfectly satisfied that no consideration save a desire to re-establish your health could induce you to leave the service, I cannot, therefore, withhold my consent. But, in giving permission to your retiring from the army, I am not only to regret the loss of a good officer, but the cause which makes his resignation necessary. When it is convenient to transmit the settlement of your public accounts, it will receive my final acceptance.

I am, &c.,
GEORGE WASHINGTON

Thus, in his 23rd year, and with the most brilliant prospects before him, Colonel Burr was compelled, by the state of his health, to retire from the army, and abandon his military career.

XIV

BURR REMOVES TO NEW YORK.—MAJOR ANDRE AND THE WIFE
OF BENEDICT ARNOLD.—MARRIAGE OF BURR.—DEATH
OF HAMILTON.—BLENNERHASSETT ISLAND.—
MRS. BLENNERHASSETT.—ARREST OF BURR.—TRIAL
AND ACQUITAL.—BURR GOES ABROAD.—DEATH AND
BURIAL OF AARON BURR.—CONCLUSION

After Colonel Burr retired from the army, he married Mrs. Theodosia Prevost, widow of a British officer who died in the West Indies. The marriage took place in 1782.

When the British evacuated New York city, Burr took up his residence there, and practised as a lawyer. Burr's wife related to him the following facts which threw some light upon the character of Mrs. Arnold, the wife of Gen. Benedict Arnold, the traitor:

"In the summer of 1780, Major Andre, of the British army, was in correspondence with Mrs. Arnold (the wife of General Arnold), under a pretext of supplying her, from the city of New York with millinery and other trifling articles of dress. On the 23rd of September, 1780, Major Andre was captured, and the treason of the General discovered. When this news reached West Point, Mrs. Arnold became, apparently, almost frantic. Her situation excited the sympathy of some of the most distinguished officers of the American army. Mrs. Arnold having obtained from General Washington a passport, and permission to join her husband in the city of New York, left West Point, and on her way stopped at the house of Mrs. Prevost; in Paramus, where she stopped one night. On her arrival at Paramus, the frantic scenes of West Point was renewed, and continued as long as strangers were present. Mrs. Prevost was known as the wife of a British officer, and connected with the royalists. In her, therefore, Mrs. Arnold could confide.

"As soon as they were alone, Mrs. Arnold became tranquilized, and assured Mrs. Prevost that she was heartily sick of the theatrics she was exhibiting. She stated that she had corresponded with the British Commander—that she was disgusted with the American cause, and those who had the management of the public affairs—and that, through great persuasion and unceasing perseverance, she had ultimately brought the General into an arrangement to surrender West

Point to the British. Mrs. Arnold was a gay, accomplished, artful, and extravagant woman.

"There is no doubt, therefore, that for the purpose of acquiring the means of gratifying an inordinate vanity, she contributed greatly to the utter ruin of her husband, and thus doomed to everlasting infamy and disgrace all the fame he had acquired as a gallant soldier at the sacrifice of his blood."

These facts were made known to Colonel Burr by Mrs. Prevost after she had became the wife of the latter, and are confirmed by the following anecdote:

"Miss Arnold was the daughter of Chief Justice Shippen of Pennsylvania. She was personally acquainted with Major Andre, and it is believed, corresponded with him previous to her marriage. In the year 1779–80, Colonel Robert Morris resided at Springatsburg, in the vicinity of Philadelphia, adjoining Bush Hill. Some time previous to Arnold's taking command of West Point, he was an applicant for the post.

"On a particular occasion, Mrs. Arnold was dining at the house of Colonel Morris. After dinner, a friend of the family came in, and congratulated Mrs. Arnold on a report that her husband was appointed to a different, but more honorable command. The information affected her so much as to produce hysteric fits. Efforts were made to convince her that the general had been selected for a preferable station.

"These explanations, however, to the astonishment of all present, produced no effect. But, after the treason of Arnold was discovered, the family of Colonel Morris entertained no doubt that Mrs. Arnold was privy to, if not negotiator for, a surrender of West Point to the British, even before the general had charge of the post."

As a lawyer, Colonel Burr was overrun with business. He proved himself a most able man at the bar, and was frequently absent on business connected with his profession.

In the autumn of 1791, Colonel Burr took his seat in the American Congress as a senator; they convened at Philadelphia. From that time forward Burr was known as an active politician, and belonged to what was called the Anti-Federal Party. In course of time Burr was elected Vice-President of the United States under Jefferson, but came very near being President. For a long time, it was doubtful which of the two would receive the majority.

According to the rules of electing President and Vice-President in those days, there were two candidates, Burr and Jefferson. The

Republican ticket prevailed, and there was a tie between the candidates, i.e., Burr and Jefferson had an equal number of votes. Therefore the House of Representatives must choose the President. The one that had the most ballots would be President, and the other would be Vice President.

The law required that the votes should be taken by States. Mr. Jefferson was the presiding officer; having opened the package of a State, he handed it to the tellers.

On opening the package endorsed Georgia votes, the tellers discovered it to be totally irregular. Mr. Wells, a teller on the part of the Senate, declared "that the envelope was blank; that the return of the votes was not authenticated by the signatures of the electors, or any of them, either on the outside or the inside of the envelope, or in any other manner; that it merely stated on the inside that the votes of Georgia were, for Thomas Jefferson four, and for Aaron Burr four, without the signature of any person whatsoever.

"Mr. Wells added that he was very undecided as to the proper course to be pursued by the tellers. It was, however, suggested by one of them that the paper be handed to the presiding officer, without any statement from the tellers, except that the return was informal; that he consented to this arrangement under the firm conviction that Mr. Jefferson would announce the nature of the informality from the chair; but, to his utmost surprise, he (Mr. Jefferson) rapidly declared that the votes of Georgia were four for Thomas Jefferson and four for Aaron Burr, without noticing their informality, and in a hurried manner put them aside, and then broke the seals and handed to the tellers the package from the next State.

"Mr. Wells observed that as soon as Mr. Jefferson looked at the paper purporting to contain a statement of the electoral vote of the State of Georgia, his countenance changed, but that the decision and promptitude which he acted on that occasion convinced him of that which he (a federalist) and his party had always doubted, that is to say Mr. Jefferson's decision of character, at least were his own interest was at hazard. Mr. Wells further stated, that if the votes of Georgia had not thus been counted, as it would have brought all the candidates into the house, Mr. Pinckney among the number, Mr. Jefferson could not have been elected president."

John Nicholas, who was also one of the tellers, made the same statement respecting the conduct of Jefferson. He was a warm personal and political friend of Jefferson, and declared that he never felt so astounded in his life as when he discovered the irregularity.

Thomas Jefferson was finally President of the United States, and Aaron Burr Vice President.

About this time Burr was charged, by his rancorous enemies, with having intrigued with the Federalists or Tories in order to supplant Thomas Jefferson and get the office of President for himself.

Burr treated all these charges with contempt, never stooping to defend himself when attacked by slanderous reports. But the individuals with whom Burr was said to have intrigued came out openly and denied the charge.

Burr's contemptuous silence, however, operated against his political character, until it became a general belief that he had intrigued, with the other party, against Mr. Jefferson, for the presidency.

Matthew L. Davis, who was intimately acquainted with Colonel Burr for the space of forty years, says:

"Through life, Colonel Burr committed an error, if he did not display a weakness, in permitting his reputation to be assailed, without contradiction, in cases where it was perfectly defensible. His enemies took advantage of the sullen silence which he was known to preserve in regard to newspaper attacks. Under these attacks he fell from the proud eminence he once enjoyed to a condition more mortifying and more prostrate than any distinguished man has even experienced in the United States.

"Different individuals, to gratify different feelings, have ascribed this unprecedented fall to different causes. But one who is not altogether ignorant of the springs of human action; whose partialities and prejudices are mellowed by more than threescore years of experience; who has carefully and laboriously, in this case, examined cause and effect, hesitates not in declaring that, from the moment Aaron Burr was elected vice-president, his own downfall was unalterably decided, if that decision could be accomplished by a combination of wealth, of talent, of government patronage, of favoritism and proscription, inflamed by the worst passions, and nurtured by the hope of gratifying a sordid ambition. The contest in Congress fixed his fate. Subsequent events were only consequences resulting from antecedent facts."

Although Colonel Burr would not deign to notice ordinary slanders and the abusive attack of the newspapers, yet when he found "a foeman worthy of his steel," he called him to a rigid account for reports circulated against his reputation.

The lamentable fate of Alexander Hamilton is a proof of this. Hamilton had endeavored to thwart the ambition of Burr by representing him as a man of no principle, and one who ought not to be trusted by the public with any responsible office.

A correspondence was opened between them by Burr, at New York, on the 18th of June, 1804. It resulted in a challenge from Colonel Burr.

The parties met at Hoboken on the 11th of July. The account of what took place on the ground is thus given by one who was present:

"Colonel Burr arrived first on the ground, as had been previously agreed. When General Hamilton arrived, the parties exchanged salutations, and the seconds proceeded to make their arrangements. They measured the distance, ten full paces, and cast lots for the choice of position, as also to determine by whom the word should be given, both of which fell to the second of General Hamilton. They then proceeded to load the pistols in each other's presence, after which the parties took their stations. The gentleman who was to give the word, then explained to the parties the rules which were to govern them in firing, which were as follows: The parties being placed at their stations, the second who gives the word shall ask them whether they are ready; being answered in the affirmative, he shall say—present! After this the parties shall present and fire when they please. If one fires before the other, the opposite second shall say, one, two, three, fire, and he shall then fire or lose his fire. He then asked if they were prepared; being answered in the affirmative, he gave the word present, as had been agreed on, and both parties presented and fired in succession.

"The intervening time is not expressed, as the seconds do not precisely agree on that point. The fire of Colonel Burr took effect, and General Hamilton almost instantly fell.

"Colonel Burr advanced towards General Hamilton with a manner and gesture that appeared to General Hamilton's friend to be expressive of regret; but, without speaking, turned about and withdrew, being urged from the field by his friend, as has been subsequently stated, with a view to prevent his being recognized by the surgeon and bargemen who were then approaching. No further communication took place between the principals, and the barge that carried Colonel Burr immediately returned to the city. We conceive it proper to add that the conduct of the parties in this interview was perfectly proper, as suited the occasion."

General Hamilton died on the day after the duel. He was interred on Saturday, the 14th of July, with military honors, the Society of the Cincinnati being charged with the funeral ceremonies of its president-general. The body was conducted to Trinity Church, where an appropriate oration was delivered by the Hon. Gouverneur Morris.

In a letter to his son-in-law, Joseph Alston, Burr wrote:

NEW YORK, July 13, 1804

General Hamilton died yesterday. The malignant federalists or tories, and the imbittered Clintonians, unite in endeavoring to excite public sympathy in his favor and indignation against his antagonist. Thousands of absurd falsehoods are circulated with industry. The most illiberal means are practised in order to produce excitement, and for the moment, with effect.

I propose leaving town for a few days, and meditate also a journey for some weeks, but whither is not resolved. Perhaps to Statesburgh. You will hear from me again in about eight days.

AARON BURR

For a considerable time after the death of General Hamilton, Colonel Burr was engaged in traveling about the country. His letters were dated in various places. Sometimes he wrote to his relatives from Savannah, sometimes from Hampton, St. Simon's, and again from Frederica; then his letters were dated at Gaston's Bluff, Fayetteville, Petersburgh, Richmond; Lexington, Kentucky, and at Nashville.

During all these wanderings, Colonel Burr was engaged in public business in one sense, but very private business in another.

There had long been a talk of separating the South American provinces from the government of Spain. Burr entered into the spirit of it, and while traveling about the Western country, he was preparing for the revolutionizing of Mexico, and for forming a settlement on what was called the Bastrop lands.

Opportunely for Burr's purpose, there was at that time serious talk of a war with Spain, and such a war would have been popular with the Western people.

General Wilkinson joined the project at first, and his troops were to be employed in the affair. General Andrew Jackson also agreed to accompany him with his whole division, if assured that Burr contemplated nothing hostile against the United States. Col. Charles Williamson, brother of Lord Balgray, went to England on the business, and, from the encouragement which he received, it was hoped and believed that a British naval squadron would have been furnished in aid of the expedition.

At this juncture Mr. Pitt died; and General Wilkinson having heard of this, became alarmed, and resolved on abandonment of the enterprise at the sacrifice of his associates.

The headquarters of Burr's operators, where his plans were talked over and matured, was Blennerhassett Island, so called for its proprietor and inhabitant, Herman Blennerhassett.

The island is in Virginia, on the Ohio River, near to Marietta.

Mr. Blennerhassett was from Ireland, was possessed of a fine estate, and lived in elegant style. His splendid house was furnished with princely elegance, and was the resort of the most intelligent and beautiful ladies in that part of the country.

It was in the summer of 1806, that a gentleman of erect carriage, but of moderate stature, arrived at Marietta, and engaged a boatman to row him over to Blennerhassett Island.

On arriving at the shore, the stranger stepped from the boat to the beach, and at the same moment a party of ladies and gentlemen came out from a covert of beautiful underwood and wild vines, and saluted him.

"Colonel, I hope you've had a pleasant voyage. We have been watching you for the past ten minutes, and congratulate you on having escaped the dangers of the seas," cried the silvery voice of a nymph of seventeen summers, who placed her little white hand in that of the officer.

"Miss Borienne, that accounts for my safety through the dangers you mention; your bright eyes were, no doubt, my protection," was the reply as the other gave his hand to several others of the company in succession as they greeted his arrival.

There was no more restraint here than the rules of good breeding required, liberally interpreted, and with laughter and other evidences of joyous hilarity, the whole troop accompanied the new comer to the lighted mansion before them.

On entering the elegant drawing-room, they were approached by a fine-looking gentleman about five feet ten inches in height, between 40 and 50 years of age. His hair curled considerably, and was, here and there streaked with gray. His eyes were full and dark, his nose a medium between the Roman and Grecian, even and fine mouth, and broad chin.

He wore a fashionable broad-collared dress coat, long waiscoat, ruffled waist-bands and shirt bosom, with snow white cravat. He also wore breeches with knee buckles, according to the fashion of that period.

"Colonel Burr, welcome; thrice welcome, for we have expected you long," cried this gentleman, embracing the new comer cordially, and looking around for his wife.

"Oh! here comes Mrs. Blennerhassett!" cried the colonel, in a tone expressive at once of joy and profound respect.

The lady who was thus addressed as Mrs. Blennerhassett was a brilliant specimen of intellectual and feminine beauty.

The complexion of Mrs. Blennerhassett was pure as the delicately tinted sea-shell, and her features perfectly regular. She had large blue eyes, very clear and of the deepest hue; her cheeks were round and generally dimpled by a most winning smile. Her hair was of a glossy brown, and very luxuriant. Her form was perfection itself. She moved lightly and gracefully, and had a foot that was at once small and beautifully shaped.

The dress of this lady was rich and neat, and worn with the grace and easy negligence which distinguished well-bred women of all countries. There was nothing masculine in her appearance: on the contrary, there was a gentleness, a softness of tone, and blandness of expression calculated to make the most humble dependant perfectly at ease in her presence.

She replied to the greeting of Colonel Burr as cordially as her husband had done. But the colonel was soon closeted with Blennerhassett himself.

"You say that the people in the vicinity continue to take a warm interest in the expedition?" said Burr.

"They are alive with enthusiasm," returned the other, "and there can be no doubt that they will flock to your standard to a man as soon as it is lifted."

Burr remained silent for a moment, and looked at Blennerhassett steadily.

"You have heard some tidings—something unexpected," said Blennerhassett, laying his hand impressively on the arm of his companion.

Burr replied by placing in the hands of Blennerhassett a letter, the seal of which was broken, and which the latter read aloud thus:

Colonel Burr,
Dear Sir

Though a stranger to you, I take the liberty of addressing you this note. Place not confidence in every one who appears friendly to your person, and favorable to your cause. By taking heed to this suggestion, you may save yourself much trouble. Those who are of an elevated rank are not always the most trustworthy.

This is from one who knows, and who has the honor to sign himself,

Your well-wisher, and obdt. servant,
JOHN SMITH

The letter was without date. Blennerhassett scrutinized the chirography a long time, in order, if possible, to discover the writer, but was obliged to acknowledge that the hand was unknown to him.

"John Smith is, doubtless, a homme de guerre," said Burr.

"Yes, colonel, the note is anonymous. Perhaps that you would act wisely to take no notice of it."

"Burr shook his head. "On occasions like the present," he said, "everything of this kind is worthy of examination and critical inquiry. The writer is evidently aware that we have an expedition in prospective."

Blennerhassett read the note again, and then observed that the writer, in speaking of persons of elevated rank, seemed to squint at Jefferson.

"Hardly," returned Burr, "for we have never confided our plans to him."

"True, sir, but he is known to be your secret enemy, and—"

"Nay, sir, that can do me no injury, unless he is made acquainted with our designs, in which case he would, doubtless, use his best efforts to crush me."

"You have some one in view, colonel," said the other, interpreting the looks of his friend.

"Pit is dead," returned Burr, "and you know how impatient some of our friends have deemed the co-operation of a British squadron."

"Ah! sits the wind in that quarter?" cried Blennerhassett, striking his forhead. He read the note again. He looked at Burr, and was silent.

"At all events, we will so far heed the hint given us," said Burr, "as to make no more disclosures to General Wilkinson."

"You have named him, sir. It is evident that the writer has his suspicions aroused by something that he has seen in the conduct of Wilkinson."

"It certainly seems so," returned Colonel Burr. "But we must wait for farther developments. In the mean time, the Catholics are in our interest and we may rely upon their aid. I have conversed with many of their bishops, as well as with many distinguished Mexican laymen. I think the country ripe for revolt, and we will not despair even if Wilkinson goes to Washington."

The two gentlemen then re-joined the company, who were, indeed, impatient to converse with the colonel.

After an hour spent in hilarity, the company scattered over the beautiful grounds surrounding the mansion, just as the full moon came up resplendent from a bed of clouds that rested on the far horizon.

By the silver light of the broad luminary, we behold a couple that have strayed far from the rest, and who now pause in the midst of a beautiful bower of nature's own forming.

The lady stopped first, and looking her companion earnestly in the face, as a moonbeam more distinctly revealed his features to her, she said in an agitated tone:

"But, colonel, what am I to understand by this language? You have told me that for my husband you entertained the most unbounded friendship, while for me—and I acknowledge that I have surpassed the bounds of prudence in permitting you so often to take these solitary rambles with me—for me, I say, you have professed a pure, disinterested regard which the seraphs themselves would sanction, and as I supposed, even that regard was grounded upon the unalterable esteem which you bore to him who has my plighted vow for life—for life."

"My dearest Mrs. Blennerhassett, how you misinterpret my words. Yon moon, which now looks down in attestation of my truth, is not more chaste, more pure than the sentiment which I feel towards you. This hand would be the first—nay I except no one—the first to strike to the earth the wretch who should charge you with any other feeling towards another than one which was in perfect consonance with your fidelity as a devoted and attached wife to my inestimable friend. Yet because I have coupled your personal graces in my imaginations with those of the heart, with the treasures of your cultivated intellect, you seem to doubt the purity of—"

"No, colonel," interrupted she, "if I really doubted the purity of your motives, you know very well that I should not be here."

"Pardon me, dear madam. Doubt is not the word: but you deem it necessary to remind me that I am only a friend."

"If anything uttered by me grated harshly on the feelings of Colonel Burr," returned the lady in a tone of much feeling, "the deep regret of both myself and Mr. Blennerhassett would plead for forgiveness."

"Then we are friends again, and may the heavens launch heaviest bolts at this head when I dream of being more—at least while your husband, my best friend, continues with us. But were you free—oh! madam! were you not the wife of another, and that other Mr. Blennerhassett, the cold formalities of friendship would pass away like the chill vapors of the night scudding before the tropical hurricane, and at your feet, I would pour out the agony that rends and consumes my heart—that your first glance kindled there. You should know what love really is."

Mrs. Blennerhassett stood transfixed, her countenance pale as the sheeted dead. For a moment she doubted the evidence of her senses. He who had just declared himself incapable of entertaining other than the most chaste and disinterested friendship for her, and had conjured the gods to crush him when he felt otherwise, had, in the same breath, declared for her the most violent passion!

She looked at Burr astonished beyond measure, while he surveyed her glorious bust, and rounded hips with the fire of passion almost scorching his veins.

Mrs. Blennerhassett was unable to speak. She knew that her husband loved Burr with fervor of devotion equal to that of Jonathan for David of old, while she entertained for the colonel the deepest respect and the most profound admiration. How could she repel his approaches as they deserved? How could she remind him of his strange inconsistancy?

"Pardon me," said Burr, at length, as if reason had resumed her sway in his distracted brain—"I am vexed beyond measure, and could cut out my tongue for betraying a secret which I had thought to carry with me to the grave. Oh! forgive me, gentlest, best, most lovely of angels! In the moment when I had resolved never—never to speak to you in any other manner than such as became our relative situations, the tide of feeling burst, tore away the flood-gate of my stern resolve. I look on you and perish, that is my history. Come, come away," continued he in a voice of heart-breaking agony (which he well knew how to assume), "for I am not myself. Your beauty—your transcendant loveliness maddens me, and distresses you. Let me die a thousand deaths rather than to cause you one pang. Let us go."

Still Burr did not go. He only turned as if about to seek their companions; but stopped again, as if unable to quit the presence of Mrs. Blennerhassett, gazing upon her charms, and sighing deeply, till, at length, he threw himself at her feet, and poured forth a torrent of the most extravagant professions.

Fully believing that Burr was the victim of an unfortunate attachment, and that her friend and her husband's friend was in danger of being driven to despair, or to the commission of some desperate act, Mrs. Blennerhassett placed her little white hands upon his brow, where her tears had first fallen plentifully, and begged him to rise.

"You will think better of this, dear colonel," said she in a tone of the deepest sympathy. "I am unworthy to give you all this unhappiness. Such a man as Colonel Burr can command the fairest in the land. Why should he trouble himself about one who had many superiors, and whose equals greet him at every step? Come, sir, I will freely overlook, and forget all that has been said."

"Yes, you will forget all that I can say," murmured Burr, regaining his feet, and supporting himself by a tree. "I should have known that when I did find a woman whom I could truly love, would hear and forget me."

"I shall never forget you, colonel; no, never. The woman or the man who has known Colonel Burr—who has been honored by his friendship—cannot forget the most remarkable man of the age."

"But she who has been disgraced by his love—ah! there, madam, is the point. You deem it a—You are offended at my presuming to love the most attractive woman of this or any other age."

"Colonel, you know my situation!"

"And, alas! thanks to my resistless passion, you know mine—the situation of Tantalus—of one of the dammed in Tartarus raising his blasted, hollow, and burning eyes to the beautified realms of endless bliss, while the brightest seraph of the heavenly band thrusts him back, as he vainly essays to climb the sides of the horrible pit, and bids him burn—burn forever in those intolerable lakes from which he may never hope to rise!"

"Oh! colonel, colonel, dear colonel! be comforted! do not say so," cried the lady, as Burr lay writhing on the ground like a wounded serpent.

"No, no. I swear," cried he, in a hollow voice, "never to rise again. Such misery as I have endured from the moment when I first saw you—"

Burr glanced towards Mrs. Blennerhassett. She leaned overpowered against a tree, her eyes glowing out from her pallid countenance "like jewels set in white marble."

Burr knew that this was the moment of weakness. Partly rising, he threw himself before her and drew her down upon the grass and wild flowers; but in such manner as if it had been a blind act of desperation on his part. He quickly removed the drapery from the limbs, and the moonbeams played upon the loveliest feminine proportions which the most fervid indignation ever conceived.

He plunged into the midst of Paradise: he tasted the sweetest draught that woman ever vouchsafed to man. He never doubted, for a moment, that Mrs. Blennerhassett had loved him long and tenderly, so delighted was she by his embrace, that she swooned in his arms.

From that time forward, the partition wall was broken down, and the colonel took his fill of love whenever he visited Blennerhassett Island.

Mr. Blennerhassett was a man of elegant taste, and several times while his lady and Burr were engaged in voluptuous pleasure, in some retired nook, on the island, they could hear the notes of Blennerhassett's flute, as he accompanied their performance with the most delightful and love-inspiring music.

On that beautiful Island, Colonel Burr spent, perhaps, the happiest portion of his life. There he met the loveliest and the gayest women and the most devoted adherents, and admirers, of his military genius.

Whispers soon began to be circulated, in the neighborhood of the island that Burr and Blennerhassett were plotting treason—that the arms of their recruits were to be turned against their own country—that Burr meditated the violent disruption of the United States.

Next came the alarming tidings that the officers of justice were about to visit the island and arrest the conspirators. They came. The leaders of the expedition fled, and their followers were scattered and disheartened.

Colonel Burr was, after a hot pursuit, discovered and arrested on the Tombigbee river, in the territory of Mississippi. He was conveyed to Richmond, Va., where he arrived on the 26th of March, 1807.

He was bailed until the 22d of May, when the court was convened for his trial. Thomas Jefferson, then President of the United States adopted every means to procure his conviction, and compass his ignominious death.

Wilkinson had received a letter in cipher from Mr. Swartwout which he first altered and then deciphered. Wilkinson swore that the translation was correct, but the grand jury discovered the forgery and compelled Wilkinson to acknowledge his guilt.

Though Mr. Jefferson knew that Wilkinson was a Spanish pensioner, and not withstanding his perjury before the grand jury, yet Mr. Jefferson sustained and countenanced him as a proper instrument by which to effect his purposes against Burr.

Other generals were arrested; but only Burr and Blennerhassett were brought on to trial.

Burr was subjected to unnumbered outrages and cruelties, but the jury brought in a verdict, thus:

"We of the jury say that Aaron Burr is not proved to be guilty under this indictment by any evidence submitted to us. We, therefore, find him not guilty."

Colonel Burr objected to this verdict as informal; and after some debate, the jury were sent back, who retired and soon after brought in a verdict of NOT GUILTY.

The excitement produced by the discovery of Burr's movements and his trial, was tremendous.

Colonel Burr soon after departed for Europe. He found some friends in England, and endeavored to interest the government in his scheme for revolutionizing the South American colonies. But the English became suspicious of this famous man, and he was obliged to cross over to the continent.

After an absence from home of four years, Colonel Burr landed in New York, where he resumed his profession and practised as a lawyer. Clients flowed in upon him, but he was always poor and encumbered with debts. He lived to the age of 81 years, and died on Staten Island whether he had been conveyed for the benefit of the pure air.

The remains of Colonel Burr were taken to Princeton, New Jersey, and intered in the college burying place near the tombs of his ancestors.

THE END

A Note About the Book

The Amorous Intrigues and Adventures of Aaron Burr (1861) is an erotic narrative of the sexual life of Aaron Burr, a leading figure in the early days of American democracy. After a distinguished career in the Continental Army, he became a lawyer and politician in New York City. From 1791 to 1797, he served as a United States Senator from the state of New York before running for president against Thomas Jefferson. When the 1800 presidential race ended in an electoral college tie, Burr was appointed Jefferson's vice president. In 1804, while serving the last year of his term, Burr shot and killed Alexander Hamilton in a duel, virtually ending his own career in politics. Over the next several decades, he traveled the frontier, avoided imprisonment on charges of treason, made more enemies than he ever had friends, and gained a reputation for womanizing and faithlessness. Published anonymously, *The Amorous Intrigues and Adventures of Aaron Burr* is an erotic biography purporting to reveal in graphic detail the sexual exploits of one of America's most infamous political leaders.

A Note from the Publisher

Spanning many genres, from non-fiction essays to literature classics to children's books and lyric poetry, Mint Edition books showcase the master works of our time in a modern new package. The text is freshly typeset, is clean and easy to read, and features a new note about the author in each volume. Many books also include exclusive new introductory material. Every book boasts a striking new cover, which makes it as appropriate for collecting as it is for gift giving. Mint Edition books are only printed when a reader orders them, so natural resources are not wasted. We're proud that our books are never manufactured in excess and exist only in the exact quantity they need to be read and enjoyed. To learn more and view our library, go to minteditionbooks.com

bookfinity & MINT EDITIONS

Enjoy more of your favorite classics with Bookfinity,
a new search and discovery experience for readers.
With Bookfinity, you can discover more vintage
literature for your collection, find your Reader Type,
track books you've read or want to read,
and add reviews to your favorite books.
Visit www.bookfinity.com, and click on
Take the Quiz to get started.

Don't forget to follow us
@bookfinityofficial and @mint_editions

9 781513 132686